THE MYSTERIOUS WU FANG:
THE CASE OF THE YELLOW MASK

THE CASE OF
THE YELLOW MASK

By Robert J. Hogan

ALTUS PRESS • 2017

CHAPTER 1
MASTER OF DEATH

THE ROOM was distinctly oriental. It was large, spacious, and had been carved out of the rock deep down below New York's Chinatown. The walls were covered with magnificent embroidered tapestries in silk and gold; even the ceiling was festooned with intricately-worked cloth.

In a luxurious bed at one end of the room, a long, slim figure wrinkled the silken covers. Regular, labored breathing came from the wide nostrils of the yellow face on the pillow. Wu Fang, the Dragon Lord of Crime, lay asleep.

Beside the bed, a heavily carved table held a more occidental-looking box with knobs and a dial. From the grating at one end of it came a gentle, humming sound, followed by words. It was a radio.

"Wu Fang! Wu Fang! Wu Fang!"

The yellow man on the bed moved restlessly, but he seemed to have difficulty in arousing himself to a full awakening.

The voice continued, "Wu Fang! Wu Fang! Wu Fang!"

With a final effort, the sleeping man succeeded in sitting up.

He stared at the instrument beside him, muttering in Cantonese.

Wu Fang didn't seem to be quite himself. His movements were slow, and from the expression on his long, yellow face, he seemed to find it difficult to think clearly. Then, quite abruptly,

"You will now be annoited for the sacrifice, Mr. Hazzard," he said.

he arrived at a decision. He reached for a knob at the corner of the carved table and turned it. There was a slight, almost inaudible click. He drew a microphone from a shelf under the table top and held it to his thin lips. He spoke into it, using a tongue of his own invention, known only to himself and his agents.

2

"You may begin," he said. "Wu Fang listens."

Immediately, the first voice began talking in the same mysterious tongue. The words were delivered slowly, as though the speaker were not accustomed to speaking in that language.

Wu Fang sat there in his bed without moving a muscle. His face was a mask of perfect calm, almost of boredom, until the other was nearly finished. Then suddenly, his eyes took on their characteristic, glowing green light. He listened intently.

Again Wu Fang spoke into the microphone. "Stay where you are," he said. "You will receive further orders directly."

Now his green, slanted eyes shifted toward the one door of the room. For while he had been speaking, the door had opened and a lovely, dark-eyed girl had entered.

He switched off the sending apparatus and stared steadily at the girl, who was shutting the door behind her.

"Ah, Mohra, my little flower," he said gently. "We leave very soon."

Mohra's dark eyes widened in surprise.

"But Wu Fang," she protested, "you are not ready to travel. Doctor Liang said that you must be very careful or infection might set in. He is here now to see you. I came to learn if you were awake yet."

The smile that had crossed the cruel, thin lips of the Dragon Lord of Crime faded a little. "You have done well in nursing me, Mohra," he said, "but that doesn't give you or Doctor Liang the right to control my destiny. As I have just said, we begin our travels as soon as possible."

"Remember, Wu Fang," Mohra persisted in her calm voice, "you were burned quite badly in the fire."

Wu Fang's eyes glowed suddenly.

"Remember it?" he breathed. "In the name of a thousand devils, how could I forget it?" His voice rose a little as it always did in anger or excitement. "Remember, my little flower, that fire was started by your friends, Val Kildare and Jerry Hazard.

There will be a reckoning with them, and when I reap my vengeance, they will believe that all the devils of hell are after them."

A frightened look came into the dark eyes of the girl as she shook her head.

"No, Wu Fang," she said, "you are wrong. They didn't start the fire. You started it yourself. Do you remember? And you gave me your word that you would not bring vengeance against them if I would nurse you back to health."

The eyes of the yellow fiend seemed to shoot green fire. "I don't believe I promised that, Mohra," he grated. "If I did, I must have been delirious. I would rather die than promise a thing like that. Val Kildare and Jerry Hazard are the only ones who have prevented me from gaining control of the world."

"Then you will not keep your promise?" Mohra asked. She trembled a little as she asked that question. But the strange eyes of Wu Fang were upon her and her anger seemed to subside before their iridescent gleam. Wu Fang answered her question with a piece of advice.

"If I ever promise to forget the past concerning Kildare and Hazard in even a small measure," he said, "you will know that I am either insane or delirious. Remember that, my little flower."

The girl stood motionless before him now. Her lips quivered for an instant, and then the muscles of her jaw bulged as her teeth clenched. The hands that hung limply at her sides tightened but only for an instant. Then she relaxed again.

"Do you understand, my little flower?" Wu Fang cooed.

Mohra nodded, ever so slowly.

"Yes," she said. "Yes, I understand." Then she added, "Doctor Liang is waiting."

Wu Fang nodded. "You may show him in."

MOHRA OPENED the door, and stepped out into a little corridor. Wu Fang heard her say, "Doctor Liang, you may come in now."

Doctor Liang was a portly Chinaman, with a round face that beamed cheerfully.

"Ah, good evening, Mister Wu," he said as he entered. "But you must not sit up. You are not quite ready for that, yet."

"You don't think so, Doctor Liang?" Wu Fang asked.

The doctor smiled tolerantly. "It is written, Mister Wu, that the well must take care, lest they grow sick; and the sick must grow well with caution, lest they grow sicker."

"That," said Wu Fang with a smile, "is applicable only to the poor unfortunates who have not the intelligence to know their own condition. I must travel as soon as possible."

Doctor Liang nodded. He spoke in the manner of one humoring a child.

"Yes, yes, of course, Mr. Wu. Perhaps in three or four days it will be safe for you to take a short journey."

"Pardon a correction," Wu Fang begged, "but in a few hours I must travel—and the journey will not be a short one. A little matter has come up that demands my immediate attention—in Peru."

Doctor Liang had just reached Wu Fang's bedside and was preparing to unwrap the bandages from the shoulders and body

Wu Fang, Dragon Lord of Crime

of the yellow fiend. Now he stopped short and stared in amazement.

"Peru!" he gasped. He stepped back a pace and looked anxiously down at the man on the bed. "But you must be insane, Mister Wu."

"On the contrary," Wu Fang assured him, "I am perfectly sane for the first time since I incurred these burns. I leave for Peru as soon as the proper arrangements can be made."

The doctor smiled and bowed graciously.

"Yes, of course," he agreed. "But in a mental state only. Perhaps you are joking, Mr. Wu."

Now the doctor stepped back to the side of the bed and began undoing the bandages once more.

"I am quite aware of the fact that I seem mad," Wu Fang admitted, "but that doesn't change my purpose."

He clapped his hands in quick succession. Whereupon a door opened noiselessly, and a squat, ugly little Chinaman glided into the room. Wu Fang spoke to him in Chinese.

"Chin Lu, you know the chemical content of my discovery known as Hilum. You will bring me a portion of it at once."

Without a word, Chin Lu bowed and glided from the room. Perhaps three minutes passed while Doctor Liang worked on, unwrapping the bandages and inspecting the body of his patient. Here and there were large, red blotches where blisters showed evidence of bad burns.

Then the door opened and Chin Lu reentered as silently as he had left. He carried a small pottery container, which he presented to Wu Fang. The yellow fiend took it in his long-nailed hands, and dismissed his servant with a short nod. There was a triumphant gleam in his eyes as he smiled at Doctor Liang.

"You, Doctor Liang," he said, "are supposed to be a man of medicine, a man of great ability in your line of work." Wu Fang chuckled. He continued. "People have given names to me, most of them uncomplimentary. It will suffice to say that I am merely a brain with a yellow body attached. But in my work, it is my good fortune to stumble upon certain things; to make discoveries and inventions that serve my purpose. And this earthen jar"—he held it a little higher for the doctor's inspection—"contains a great agent, one that I have named Hilum. It was developed for another purpose, but has proven more satisfactory as a healing agent."

Doctor Liang continued with his work, smiling and nodding in a patronizing manner. It was obvious that he was convinced that Wu Fang was indeed very mad. And this fact was very plain to Wu Fang himself, who went on, "You are about to receive quite a shock, Doctor Liang. The contents of this jar will not only serve as a cure for my burns, but will also prove that now for the first time since my injuries were inflicted, I am quite sane again. You see, I was not sane before or I would have thought of this remedy at once and hence saved myself much pain. I am once more Wu Fang, the Master Mind."

With a long, yellow hand he removed the stopper from the jar. He poured a little of the thick, brownish liquid on his fingertips.

"Observe carefully the reaction, Doctor Liang," he counseled.

He rubbed the liquid very lightly upon one of the burned

portions of his chest. A bubbling, boiling process was taking place there upon his blistered skin, not unlike the combination of acid and alkali. A thin vapor was escaping, a vapor that had a pungent, medicinal odor.

Wu Fang tilted his head and addressed the doctor: "It would be well not to permit a large amount of that vapor to pass into your nostrils until the reaction has taken place and the air has assimilated it."

The doctor moved away obediently, his eyes still glued to the spot on Wu Fang's chest where the liquid was still bubbling and boiling.

"I think," Wu Fang remarked with a sly smile on his thin lips, "that I can read your thoughts, Doctor Liang. You are thinking that this liquid will burn me even worse than before. But you are wrong. The only sensation I receive is a cool, soothing feeling. And now, you see, the action is nearly completed and there's a slight, white crust formed on the skin."

As he spoke, he brushed the white, powdery substance from his chest and chuckled to himself. Doctor Liang leaped forward, staring in amazement.

"Mr. Wu," he exclaimed, "the place where you anointed yourself with this strange liquid is completely healed!"

Wu Fang chuckled as he said, "To be sure. And you, Doctor Liang, are the one who thought a moment ago that I was insane. What do you think now?"

"I think," Doctor Liang admitted quite frankly, "that this is the most marvelous cure I have ever seen. Never in all my experience as a doctor of medicine have I experienced so sudden and complete a cure for burns. It is incredible. We of the medical profession must have this substance for our use."

WU FANG'S chuckling ended. He shook his head negatively. "No," he said, "I am very sorry, but this—" he tapped the earthen jar—"is my invention and my secret. Perhaps some day, if necessary, I will offer it to the medical profession and to the world, as a ransom."

At this point, the yellow fiend bowed to Doctor Liang. "And now, Doctor Liang, since you have seen the great healing power of my Hilum; and since I am quite capable of applying it myself, I will bid you good evening. I will have no further need of your assistance."

Doctor Liang hesitated. Then he bowed low, "Very well, Mr. Wu. I will go, if you wish."

Wu Fang held up one hand to restrain the doctor. "Perhaps," he said, "a word of advice would go well here. I assume you realize the penalty for mentioning my name or my whereabouts outside the proper circles, Doctor Liang."

The Chinese doctor stiffened and gave a short nod of assent.

"I—I understand," he said in a hollow voice. "And now you wish me to go?"

"Yes," nodded Wu Fang. "Good evening."

When the doctor had left, he called Mohra to his side. He was chuckling. "Doctor Liang seemed greatly amazed, did he not, my little flower?"

Mohra nodded affirmatively but didn't reply. Wu Fang handed her the earthen jar.

"You will anoint me with the contents of the jar," he instructed her. "One burn at a time, however. The vapor it gives off is not conducive to health."

Without a word, the girl took the jar and followed her master's directions. Wu Fang clapped his hands three times. A slim, dark-skinned Asiatic, dressed in occidental costume, with a bearing not unlike that of a Hindu, entered instantly.

"You will charter a plane," Wu Fang ordered. "We fly at once to Peru. Wan Ti has just sent a report. The plane will make its first stop at Mexico City. It must be a large one, perhaps a transport. See that you get a pilot who will fly us out of the country without passports. They would be rather inconvenient. Make the arrangements at once, Kumar."

The Hindu bowed and vanished immediately. Now Wu Fang talked to Mohra as she continued to treat his burns.

"We have failed before, my little flower," Wu Fang said, "but this time we shall be successful. Wan Ti made a very interesting report this morning. He has discovered something I have been hunting for some time—the yellow mask of Unga. Unga was the ruler of what is now known as Peru, long before the Incas held sway there. He ruled with a mask of gold."

Mohra stepped back while the acrid fumes rose from the boiling liquid. She looked bewildered.

"What do you mean?" she ventured. "How could he rule with a gold mask? It doesn't make sense."

Wu Fang smiled. "I have an idea concerning it, but I don't care to mention it at this time. If I am correct in my assumption, the wearer of this mask will be all powerful. You, of course, cannot understand, but there were mysteries in those days that have never been fathomed by anyone. I will have that mask before many days have passed, my little flower, and when it is mine, you shall be the—"

A knock sounded on the door. For an instant, Wu Fang looked distressed. Then he said gently, "You may come in, Kumar."

The Hindu glided into the room. His face was troubled as he bowed before his master.

"I have been unsuccessful, Master," he said.

Wu Fang frowned as Kumar continued. "I find there are no pilots who will fly us out of the country without the proper credentials. We must leave by some other means."

Wu Fang's jaw clenched for a moment. Then he relaxed, as though he had come abruptly to a decision.

"Very well," he said. "This is the work of my two enemies, but we will outwit them." His savage green eyes were riveted upon Mohra's face. "First send my agents for Jerry Hazard and Val Kildare. We must get them out of the way definitely before we go on. Then, I will make other plans for getting out of the country and going to Peru."

He nodded with finality to Kumar, who slipped noiselessly from the room. Then he smiled at Mohra.

"I am sparing you this time, my little flower. I will not make you ferret out Kildare and Hazard. If my agents have followed my orders, they know where they can be found at any moment. I am afraid I could not trust you to the extent of sending you after them anymore. But perhaps when they are out of the way, I can have full confidence in you again. If you were not so beautiful and if you were not my little flower, you would go the way of others who have been under suspicion."

Mohra did not answer. Her face was ashen white.

CHAPTER 2
THE CREATURE ON THE ROOF

F OR TWO days, three men had occupied a private fishing camp on the shore of Long Island. The camp was the secret rendezvous of Captain Falstaff. He was a long, lean, alert man who had made himself famous during the World War and had further distinguished himself with the Secret Service in the art of decoding messages. At that very moment he was taking a few days' rest from his responsibilities as chief of the deciphering department of the federal bureau.

Two friends had joined him on his fishing trip. One was Val Kildare, former ace investigator with the federal government. The other was Jerry Hazard, international newspaper correspondent for the McNulty Syndicate.

The three men sat in the living room of their small lodge on Long Island Sound. Jerry Hazard glanced at his watch and said, "Kildare, if it wasn't for the fact that you keep me in a jumpy frame of mind, I would say that it was time to go to bed. It's nearly eleven and we've had a heavy day of fishing."

Kildare turned his head and the slightest trace of a smile played on his lips.

"Well, why don't you go to bed, Jerry? I would join you myself, but"—the broad, slim shoulders shrugged—"well, I think I'll stay up a little longer."

"You know why I don't go to bed," Hazard retorted almost reproachfully. "I'm dead tired, but there's no sense in going to bed if you're going to see all sorts of things the minute you close your eyes."

"Oh, come now, Hazard," Kildare advised. "Remember, this is only a suspicion of mine. It's a pretty strong one, I'll admit, but still it's only a suspicion.

"In the first place, I didn't like the looks of that cab driver who brought us out here. Did you notice his face and compare it with the picture on the license card?"

"No," Hazard confessed, "I didn't. As a matter of fact, I don't go in for studying cab drivers' faces."

Kildare's smile broadened. "While we're still on the trail of Wu Fang, you might find it worthwhile. If you'd done that during the last week, you would have found that the drivers of at least three cabs didn't have faces that matched the pictures on their licenses."

"Meaning, of course," Hazard shot back, "that you believe we're being followed in every move we make. I've heard you say that at least a half dozen times in the last week."

"Yes," Kildare said, nodding, "and each time I've become more firmly convinced. Let's go back to the fellow who brought us out here two days ago. As I recall, he was rather small, but I should say from what I could see of his muscles under his coat that he was quite powerful.

"He was dark-skinned and he had eyes that slanted a little

at the corners. His cheek bones were wide. All those things might possibly fit into the picture, but not the straight, black, coarse hair under his cap. He spoke with an accent, very faint, to be sure, but certainly not that of a Brooklynite. It was more Indo-Chinese. Add that to the fact that the head and shoulders of the man on the license card were those of a heavy man with Hebrew features and a round, full face—and there is something fishy in the deal."

Their host, Captain Falstaff, chuckled softly. "Well, after all, Kildare," he said, "that fishy part is quite fitting, don't you think, considering the purpose of our trip?"

Hazard moved uneasily in his chair. The thought of being in the wilds of Long Island in a fishing camp was not to his liking. Particularly when Kildare continued to speak in vagaries.

"Confound it, Kildare," he blurted out at length, "why don't you tell us what you've got on your mind so we'll know what to avoid? Here's a perfectly swell evening wasted. We might have sat outside, but you insisted on our coming into the cabin."

"It's close and stuffy in a coffin, too," Kildare reminded him. "We've been followed. First, there was the taxi driver who brought us out here. Then I have heard strange noises in the woods. Both days, when we've been fishing in the Sound, a small cruiser has kept us in full view. As a matter of fact, I wouldn't be surprised if someone were listening at one of the windows right now."

Hazard got up from his chair and walked back and forth.

"I suppose," he said, puffing hard on his cigarette, "all this means that you think our old friend, Wu Fang, is still alive and camping on our trail."

"I haven't the slightest doubt of it," Kildare admitted.

"But look here," Hazard said. "Wu Fang was in a mass of flames the last time we saw him." The suspense was wearing on Hazard.

Jerry Hazzard

KILDARE NODDED, but did not speak. Hazard continued to pace back and forth. Suddenly, he whirled, defiantly.

"All right, then," he said, "suppose Wu Fang is alive and suppose he is following us. Why doesn't he come on and get it over with?"

"That part," Kildare told him, "is as much a mystery to me as it is to you. We have been followed, but I haven't the slightest idea why the yellow devil hasn't tried to finish us off. Perhaps he wants to use us as he did in the case of the scarlet feather."

Meanwhile, Captain Falstaff was standing before a large radio at the side of the room. Now and then he turned the dials and listened. Strange music, interspersed with words in foreign languages, came drifting out of the ether.

"I never saw anyone enjoy a radio as you do," Kildare commented by way of changing the subject.

Falstaff smiled, "It isn't the radio as much as the programs I can get over the shortwave. I had this set made especially for me, and I've tuned in practically every shortwave station in the world, at one time or another. It's very interesting, particularly in my work, because it gives me an opportunity to listen to a great many languages."

"That's right," Kildare said. "But I thought you were taking a vacation up here for a few days."

"In my work," Falstaff replied, "you can never take a vacation. You've got to keep right up to the minute if you want to be in a position to decipher strange codes."

"I remember one very fine job you did during the war," Kildare said, "but I have never quite understood how you accomplished it."

"What was that?" Hazard asked eagerly, glad to rid his mind of the vague fears that tortured him.

"You tell him," Kildare said to Captain Falstaff. "I'm apt to get it all mixed up."

Captain Falstaff sat back and lighted his pipe. He lowered the radio volume.

"I was working on some codes in France," he began, "when we started to pick up messages by wireless, apparently sent by the enemy. They didn't conform with our deciphering codes and we were left pretty much in the dark as to their meaning.

So I went to work on them from the old rule for the frequent use of certain characters. It wasn't long before I had the whole thing worked out. We learned from these messages that the Germans were sending their information out in a Japanese code.

"And what the newspaper boys thought strangest of all was the fact that I didn't know a thing about the Japanese tongue. You see, it was all quite—"

Suddenly, his words were cut off as though by an ax. The faint hum from the loudspeaker was being broken now by faint sounds coming from afar. As they grew louder, the men realized that a name was being repeated over and over again, a name that made them freeze in their tracks.

"Wu Fang! Wu Fang! Wu Fang!"

"Good Lord!" Kildare breathed.

Hazard was still standing as that name echoed through the room. He stopped as though he were a statue. Icy fingers clutched him as the repetition of that name continued. "Wu Fang! Wu Fang! Wu Fang!"

He glanced significantly at Kildare with his lips parted, but remained silent.

"Wu Fang! Wu Fang! Wu Fang!"

The only one who moved was Captain Falstaff. He whirled to the table, snatched up a pencil. He drew a blank sheet of paper before him. He was poised and ready, waiting for the message that was to come.

Suddenly, the calling of the name ceased and there was a slight clicking sound in the loudspeaker. It was followed by a few words in strange jargon that none of the three had ever heard before. It was oriental, to be sure, with a spattering of other tongues thrown in.

CAPTAIN FALSTAFF'S pencil was moving rapidly across his paper. There were no words that were intelligible to Hazard. The return conversation in the weird tongue lasted for only a moment.

Meanwhile, Kildare had leaped from his seat and was walking on tiptoe to the radio. As the words ceased, he gave a short nod.

"That's Wu Fang's voice," he said hoarsely. "I'd know it anywhere." He shot a glance to the other side of the room. "You see, I was right," he said.

"Sssh!" Captain Falstaff whispered. His pencil had stopped moving and he was staring at the message he had set down on the paper. The room grew deadly quiet as he attempted to decipher it.

Suddenly, a sound came to them, not from the radio, but a scraping sound from outside. As Hazard heard that, his very blood seemed to be turning to ice water. He stood like a man in a trance, listening, trying to locate that noise. Kildare was listening, too, but Captain Falstaff seemed oblivious to everything except his work.

Scrape! Scrape! Scrape!

The sound attracted Jerry Hazard's attention to the corner of the building nearest the radio set. It wasn't a constant noise. It was moving up, up, ever so stealthily, toward the spot where the eaves of the roof fell over the wall of the building.

Kildare reached for his gun as another voice came from the

radio. Hazard seemed trans-fixed in the center of the room, listening and staring as Captain Falstaff's pencil moved like lightning across the paper, setting down the strange, garbled words as they

Val Kildare

came to him. The words ran on and on, while that stealthy movement outside continued.

Hazard's very flesh was tingling with the ominous movement. His guess was that a wildcat was climbing up the side of the building. Now it was on the roof. He could hear the boards over his head moaning gently.

Creak! Creak! Creak!

At the same time, Val Kildare hissed, "Someone's on the roof!"

Captain Falstaff didn't pay any attention to that. He merely warned them to be silent and his pencil moved faster than ever.

Kildare stepped back with his automatic in hand and stared at the roof that slanted directly over the room they were in. There was a faint creak from above. Instantly, Kildare raised his gun and fired twice. Two holes appeared in the roof as the room was filled with the deafening reports. There came a sound like that of a heavy body falling.

Scrape! Scrape! Scrape!

Something was dragging on the roof now. Then suddenly, the voice in the loudspeaker stopped short.

Captain Falstaff's voice, low but sharp, came across the room. "They got the aerial," he said. "Stay where you are. Don't move. I want to get this worked out before—"

Falstaff worked furiously to translate those sounds into English.

"Wu Fang made one error," he commented. "He answered his agent in the code tongue, and from that I'm beginning to work out the rest. You see, here are several words at the beginning of the message. When Wu Fang answered the call, there were a number of things he might have said, but these are his exact words in English: 'You may begin. Wu Fang listens.' From that I'm working out the rest of the message."

Suddenly they were startled at a thrashing sound from almost over their heads. It seemed as though something were tumbling down the side of the roof; flopping and rolling as it went. Then the lights in the cottage went out. Pitch darkness shrouded the cabin.

For an instant, Hazard was petrified. He visualized all sorts of things coming at him, tiny beasts, reptiles—

"A light!" he gasped. "Somebody strike a light!"

He felt in his pocket for his matches but before he could get them out, Kildare had snapped on his cigar lighter. For a moment, everything was as still as the grave. Then Hazard heard a rattling. He dove into his pocket for his gun and leaped to the door.

"Somebody's coming in that door!" he shouted.

In his haste, he slammed against the form of a man. His first impulse was to pull the trigger of the automatic and pour lead into whomever might be trying to enter the cabin; but for some unknown reason, he hesitated. It was fortunate, indeed, for suddenly a light flared in his face and Kildare barked, "Don't shoot. It's me. I'm locking the door."

Captain Falstaff was still sitting at the table as he struck a match. He arose and took a candle from the mantelpiece. The taper glowed and cast eerie shadows about the cabin as he set it on the table and went furiously to work again.

Kildare grasped Hazard and pointed to a chair in the far corner of the room.

"Sit down there, Jerry," he suggested, "and keep your eyes peeled on these two windows at the front of the room. If anybody appears, let them have it."

Then the federal man took a position on the other side of the room with his back to the door, facing the two windows on the opposite side.

Minutes passed, long minutes that seemed like hours, while the candle flame danced, silhouetting the three men against the walls in huge, grotesque shapes.

Hazard glanced at his watch. It should be almost dawn now, he thought, but no, his imagination was playing tricks on him. The watch showed but two minutes before midnight. Wouldn't this suspense ever end? Wouldn't Captain Falstaff ever get that message decoded? But then, Falstaff would be lucky if he got it decoded by dawn. Dawn. Hazard shuddered at the thought. Six hours to wait for action. If they could only—Hazard put his thoughts into words, "Good Lord, have we got to sit here all night? Can't we do something? What about that—"

"Just be patient a few minutes more," Captain Falstaff soothed him. "I'm nearly through."

Another long minute passed while the captain worked on. Hazard glanced at his watch again. Exactly midnight.

At that very moment, the still air outside and within was shattered by a piercing scream, a scream that came from outside the fishing camp.

"Help, Captain! Help! Help!"

CHAPTER 3
INVISIBLE WINGS

A N UNCONTROLLABLE exclamation left the lips of Jerry Hazard. Captain Falstaff leaped from his chair and lunged toward the door.

"Good heavens!" he exclaimed. "That's a woman. That's Mrs. Beemer. I know her voice."

Falstaff tried to unbolt the door, but Kildare blocked him.

"If you value your life, don't go out there," he cautioned the captain.

Falstaff glared. "Don't try to tell me what I can do in my own house," he retorted. "I tell you, it's Mrs. Beemer and she's not far away. Something's happened to her."

As he spoke, the shriek came again, louder and longer, and ending in a bloodcurdling, choked-off sob. Falstaff and Kildare faced each other by the door. They were of a size, but Falstaff was more powerful. He grasped Kildare by the shoulders, braced himself, and flung the federal man aside. Then he wrenched the door open and plunged out into the night.

A split second too late, Kildare recovered his balance and lunged after him. He stepped out of the doorway and called, but the only answer was the sound of the captain's footsteps running down the path into the inky blackness.

Hazard raced up, "What is it?"

Kildare ignored him; he kept calling, "Come back! Come back, Falstaff!"

But the secret service man paid no heed. They heard his footsteps diminish as he raced on.

"Who is this Mrs. Beemer?" Hazard demanded.

"She lives on a farm a little way from here," Kildare said hurriedly. "She's the one who baked that pie we had for dinner. Falstaff buys butter, eggs, and pastry from her when he's up here."

Jerry Hazard whirled and started down the path but Kildare stopped him.

"Wait, man," he said. "Do you want to die? At least we've got to be properly armed before we go out there."

"I've got my gun," Hazard retorted. "We can't let Falstaff go to his death without doing something to save him."

25

Kildare dragged him back inside the cabin. "I tell you we can't go without being properly armed. Your gun won't be any good in combating what's out there in the night."

Inside the cabin, Kildare jerked a couple of heavy, rustic walking sticks that stood in a rack behind the door.

"There's one of these for each of us," he said. "Grasp the small end in your hand and use the other as a club if anything comes at you. Let's hope we'll be able to hear it if it does. And here's an electric torch I found on the mantel."

Kildare thrust the light in Hazard's hand and they raced down the path. The sounds of Captain Falstaff's footsteps had died away. Hazard was about to raise his voice and call out for him when they heard his shout.

"Mrs. Beemer! Mrs. Beemer! Where are you? I'm coming."

"Look out! Here it comes again!"

Almost instantly, they heard a shot ring out in the night and saw a spurt of flame shoot from among the trees. A low cry came on the tail of that shot, rising to an ear-splitting shout of terror.

"Back!" yelled Falstaff. "Get back! It's after me!"

Hazard and Kildare were halfway between the cabin and the place where the shouting was coming from. Kildare hissed a warning to Hazard as they raced on.

"Keep your stick ready. Hurry! I'm afraid we're too late."

The beams of the electric torches slashed the darkness, revealing a winding path skirted with tall trees. Kildare ran ahead as the trail was too narrow for them to run abreast. After a moment, he raised his light, spotted it in the branches of the trees. At the same time he swished the club about his head.

Hazard, too, was slashing with his club; but he couldn't tell for the life of him what he was trying to beat down. He saw Kildare spin around and jerk out his automatic.

Blam! Blam! Blam!

Kildare's gun barked out three staccato reports in the night. Then the government man growled angrily, "Confound it, I missed."

In the next instant, they were bending over a still form lying on the ground.

"I think it's—" Kildare began. "Yes, it is Falstaff. Roll him over and take a look at him, Jerry, while I watch for the thing to come back."

AS JERRY HAZARD bent down over the limp form, his whole back felt prickly and cringing. He rolled the corpse over grimly.

"Good Lord!" he gasped. "It's Falstaff, all right."

Falstaff's eyes seemed to be fairly bulging out of their sockets, staring upward. His mouth was open and his tongue was lolling out one side. What caught Hazard's attention was the throat; it was a mass of blood and torn flesh.

"What happened to him?" Kildare asked hoarsely.

"I—I don't know," Hazard gulped. "Something got at his throat. It's torn to ribbons and there's blood all over the place. Wait, I'll test his heart action."

"There's no use," Kildare said. "I know that without looking. Captain Falstaff is dead. Look out! Here it comes again!"

For Jerry Hazard, the whole woods were filled with horrible apprehension. It seemed that every branch that caught his eye moved ominously, and that phantom shapes were plunging down at him. He could hear a low, gentle swish of wings, but he couldn't tell from what direction it came. The creature swooped at them for a second. Then it vanished.

"Keep your eyes open for it to dive again," Kildare said. "It'll be back. I want to have a look at Falstaff and then we've got to get out of here."

Hazard turned his light into the trees while Kildare dropped to the ground beside the captain's body. He realized now that he was shaking in every limb. A good, open fight was not so bad, but the idea of merely hearing a sound and then beating frantically at thin air was too much for him.

Kildare spoke. "He's dead, all right, poor devil. The Bureau is losing one of the best men it ever had. That throat is horrible. I think I see how it was done, too."

He paused for a moment, still looking down at the body. Suddenly, he let out a warning cry.

"Look out!" he yelled. "Here it comes again! For the love of heaven, beat the air!"

Jerry Hazard heard that sound, too, a gentle swishing of air passing over wings. Now he glanced up. A winged, feathered thing was hurtling toward them in the dim light. It came with such terrific speed that he couldn't see it very clearly.

The winged murderer wasn't flapping its wings now; it was sailing. Hazard ducked instinctively as it rushed him, and there was mortal desperation in the way he flung his club about. The thing tried to tear through the barrage of blows.

Kildare whirled and ran a few paces as the feathered demon zoomed upward, vanishing in the darkness. The federal agent snatched some brush from the ground. Leaf mold came up in a shower, and as it spread over Hazard, he cringed, as though phantom fingers had touched him.

"Here," Kildare ordered, "bury your face and shoulders in this. I don't think that winged devil can get through it. Hold it so the branches stick out in every direction from your face."

"But you," Hazard gasped, "what are you going to do, Kildare?"

"I've got another branch here for myself," Kildare shot back. "Now run for the cabin as fast as—"

He stopped short and stared past Hazard, who had gone a few paces up the path. An involuntary cry of alarm escaped his lips as he peered ahead. Flames leaped and crackled from the spot where the cabin had been.

"The cabin!" he shouted. "It's on fire!"

He dashed past Hazard and raced down the winding path.

Hazard followed. As they came to a turn, they could see the cabin clearly in the light of the blaze.

Jerry remembered many things as he raced down the path. He remembered that Captain Falstaff had remarked on the dryness of the woods. He had said that they must be careful about dropping matches or the whole woods would go up in flames. And now the truth of his words was apparent. The cabin was dry as tinder. One end of it was completely in flames. Smoke poured from the one door in front and billowed out in little streams from cracks about the eaves and gables.

"Stay where you are," Kildare shouted. "I'm going in to get it. Don't try to follow me. Watch out for that winged devil."
VAL KILDARE plunged headlong into the cloud of smoke that rushed from the half-open doorway. Loyalty drew Hazard after him, but a flame licked out and scorched his face, throwing him back, helpless. The flames covered the whole front of the building now, and cut Kildare off from him.

He reeled as he tried to catch his balance.

"Kildare!" he shouted. "Are you all right? Come back out of there. You'll be burned to a crisp."

The next instant his foot caught in something and he lost his balance completely. As he sprawled headlong, the automatic and other objects clattered to the ground and his empty fingers clutched at something else. Something there on the ground beneath him; something that was flesh and bone.

A breeze brushed the smoke away for an instant, and he saw the horrible figure of a man. The face was that of a Chinese with slant eyes and yellow skin, but the clothing was occidental and smeared at the stomach with big blotches of blood.

Long, powerful hands grappled with him, trying to reach his throat. A short time before, Jerry Hazard might have been an easy prey in those powerful arms, but now most of the Mongolian's strength had ebbed with the loss of blood.

Desperation and panic were driving Hazard's fingers into the naked throat of the Chinaman; they sank deeper and deeper into that yellow flesh. The Chinaman relaxed abruptly, and his hands groped in his pockets, came out again with a long, thin needle.

In spite of the fact that he was choking and gasping, the hand that held the needle moved very swiftly. Hazard managed to roll away from it, and as he did so his left hand left the yellow throat and grabbed the wrist that held the needle, pinioning it to the ground. His right came up with his fist doubled, and he slammed home a blow that smacked the yellow face between the eyes. The body beneath him went limp.

Smoke and flame were still billowing from the door as Hazard leaped to his feet and snatched up the automatic and the light.

"Kildare," he shouted. As though in answer, he heard a window crash at the rear of the cabin. Kildare shouted back hoarsely, "Come this way!" Hazard had started around the corner of the burning building when he heard something else, something far more ominous than the crackle of flames. That gentle swish of wings. He ducked and snatched up the branches he had used before against the winged demon.

Holding them so as to completely cover the upper part of

The Bird of Death

his body, he dashed around the blazing cabin. The sound came closer. Next, there was a sudden, high-pitched scream of terror—and the winged thing was gone.

As he reached the rear of the building, he saw something rolling on the ground, something that was burning—and he knew that it was Val Kildare. With one leap, he pounced upon him. Kildare's clothes were on fire; he was rolling over and over on the grass in a frantic effort to smother the fire. Hazard dropped prostrate upon him and extinguished the flame. Then the two men dashed headlong toward the shore.

"Kildare," Hazard panted, "are you all right?"

"Yes," Kildare choked. "I think so."

"Did you get the message?"

"Right," Kildare nodded. "I pulled my coat up over my face for protection. Quick now! Into the cruiser. Heaven help us if this motor doesn't start."

They ran out on the dock and leaped into the afterdeck of the small fishing cruiser. The flames from the house lighted the waterfront so clearly that they required no other light.

Hazard noticed that the door of the cabin was open. There's something wrong there, he thought; Falstaff always closed the door when he left the cruiser. He was about to investigate it, when his attention was diverted by something else. A half-naked brown form that had been lying prostrate on the cabin deck leaped from all fours, an ugly-looking knife gleaming in his hand. The powerful arm swerved lightning-fast to strike.

"Look out!" Hazard yelled to Kildare. The government man whirled and ducked. His two arms shot in the air as he stepped closer to the leaping form and the long, lean hands caught his descending wrist.

Kildare wrenched the brown arm so that it came down backward with the elbow across his shoulders. He gave it a terrific jerk. The crack of bones snapping was nearly muffled by the screams of pain and the clatter of a shimmering steel knife dropping to the deck. The brown body somersaulted into the water. With the splash, Kildare turned to follow Hazard, who moved nearer the cabin door.

Suddenly it thrust open and another brown-skinned figure leaped at them. It seemed a twin to the first attacker. He had been lying on the deck of the cabin beside the upturned dinghy.

A knife gleamed in his hand as he charged up the steps and came at Kildare's back.

HAZARD'S AUTOMATIC leaped up. He didn't bother to aim, but shot from the hip, pulling the trigger three times. *Blam! Blam! Blam!*

The automatic spat flame and found its mark. With a horrible cry the native crashed to the deck.

The body still writhed and twisted, but Kildare paid no attention to it. He stepped over it and leaped for the cruiser's starter button.

"Watch the shore, Jerry," he yelled. "I have a notion there's more of them around."

The motor caught and sputtered. It ran fitfully and then churned steadily.

"Cast off your line on the stern," Kildare shouted. "I'll get the one up ahead."

The lines were cast, the motor roared, and Kildare shoved the gear lever into forward position. The cruiser shot out into the Sound. Hazard still stared at the shore with his automatic cocked. He saw something move, took careful aim and fired, but there were no screams to tell that his bullet had struck home.

"Look out!" Kildare yelled. "There's that flying devil again! Duck into the cabin!"

As he spoke, Kildare dived down the passageway. Above the throb of the engines, they could hear the whir of wings. A shadowy form came from the trees overhanging the water. Hazard followed Kildare into the passageway with such haste that he landed on all fours in the cabin. Kildare slammed the door behind him and turned on the lights. The cruiser ploughed rapidly through the swells into the Sound.

"Keep back against that door," Kildare warned.

As he spoke, Hazard heard a flapping of wings outside. He could see a feathered thing through the little window in the cabin door. It beat furiously against the glass. Raising his automatic, he took aim.

Blam!

"What was that?" Kildare demanded.

"The bird," Hazard snapped. "I think I got it."

"Let's hope so," Kildare said. "Here." He gave Hazard the stub end of a fishing pole. "I'm going to clean house. Get ready to kill anything that moves. One of Wu Fang's devils has been in here and there's no telling what he may have left."

Hazard's flesh began to crawl as he watched the government man tear the interior of the cabin apart. Any moment, one of those vile little beasts that Wu Fang used as executors, might leap from a hidden spot.

Kildare jerked the cushions from the bunks and beat about the walls with his stick to frighten out any tiny reptiles or hybrid lizards that might have been planted there.

The curtain on the cabin door swung in the breeze, as the cruiser ploughed through the Sound, and brushed Hazard's ear. The newspaper reporter tensed, ducked instinctively.

"What was that?" Kildare asked.

"Just the curtain," Hazard said in a tremulous voice.

"Let's have a look at it," Kildare snapped. He tore the curtain away and shook it violently. "No, there's nothing there. Maybe this is a wild goose hunt, but we've got to make sure. Wu Fang strikes suddenly."

He continued beating the interior of the cabin as Hazard watched him curiously with his back to the door. A cobweb hanging from the beams above caught his eyes. He opened his mouth to cry out but then realized what it was and began laughing rather hysterically.

Kildare had covered the whole cabin without a discovery. "THERE DOESN'T seem to be anything here," he remarked with a shrug. "We might as well go on deck again. We've got to work fast."

Got to work fast. That seemed funny to Hazard. He had just begun to think they were at last reaching a point of safety.

"You mean we've got to begin pulling for New York?" he demanded.

"That's important," Kildare admitted, "but not as important as something that has got to be done before that. Come on deck and give me a hand." Hazard opened the door to step out, but Kildare warned, "Take it easy. We're not sure of that bird yet. Let me go first."

The cruiser had been traveling at top speed ever since leaving the fishing camp and was now far out in the Sound. The blazing cabin was a red glow back on the shoreline.

"It's OK," Kildare said. "I can't see any sign of that feathered killer. Come on. We're going to lower the dinghy tender."

"I don't get you," Hazard said.

"You will before long," Kildare assured him, "and then it may be too late."

He pointed to the shore from where a black speck seemed to be coming.

"See that?"

Hazard nodded.

"Well, that's the same high-speed cruiser that's been trailing us every time we've gone fishing," Kildare told him. "But they aren't merely trailing us now. They're going to try to catch us."

"Can't we turn them off and run for it?" Hazard suggested.

Kildare shook his head. "No," he said, "they've got us spotted. We're more then halfway over to Connecticut now. We're going to get a little closer to the shore and then put off in the dinghy and open the cruiser up wide. You're near the controls, Jerry. Reach down and throttle the motor back."

Hazard followed orders. Then he came back to Kildare.

"Over she goes into the water," Kildare said.

They heaved the dinghy tender over the side; it landed with a splash.

"Good," said Kildare. "Now we're close to the Connecticut shore. You loop the rope around one of the mooring stays and hang on. Keep close to the stern because I'm going to climb aboard."

Hazard climbed into the tender and held it close to the cruiser's stern. The cruiser turned abruptly toward New York, and the lights went out. The engine roared as Kildare pushed the throttle ahead again.

Jerry Hazard hung on for dear life while Kildare crawled into the tender.

"OK," Kildare said. "Let go of the rope now."

Hazard released his hold, and the cruiser shot away, nearly capsizing the tender as the break was made. Kildare manned the oars and turned toward the shore.

"Now watch that cruiser of ours heading for New York, if you want to see some fun," he advised. He pulled hard for the north shore. They watched the other boat race across the Sound, heading west. They could hear its motor and the throbbing of the more powerful motor of the other craft pursuing it.

Suddenly, there was a loud report and a flash from across the water. In the light, they saw the cruiser they had abandoned burst into a thousand pieces.

"You see, Jerry," Kildare smiled, "we might have been in that boat. I hope Wu Fang and his agents are satisfied. How surprised that yellow devil is going to be when he finds we're not as much out of the way as he thinks!"

CHAPTER 4
DEATH STRIKES

I F JERRY HAZARD and Val Kildare had any idea that Wu Fang considered the matter closed, so far as their lives were concerned, they were mistaken. Certain happenings at the fishing camp were obvious.

The man on the roof of the shack had been one of Wu Fang's special agents sent to destroy his enemies. Through the window, he had heard the message over the shortwave radio; had climbed on the roof to pull down the aerial, only to be shot by Kildare. In falling he had crashed into the electric wires joining the corner of the camp, and broken them, hence putting out the lights in the place. And it had been the same wires sputtering blue flame on the ground that ignited the building. The farm woman, Mrs. Beemer, had obviously been snatched from her bed and dragged near the camp by Wu Fang's agents so that her screams would draw their attention. As a result, Falstaff had been killed instead of Kildare.

After docking the tender at an East River pier, Hazard and Kildare took a cab to the latter's apartment. It was nearly three in the morning when they pulled up before the apartment building. The street seemed deserted. But as they descended from the taxi, a portly figure detached itself from a shadowy niche and came toward them with the short, quick step peculiar to Orientals.

Kildare stopped short. His hand touched Hazard. But the newspaperman had already spotted the Chinaman. He felt Kildare move slightly as his hand dove for his gun. The stout man was near them now and addressed them in perfect English.

"One of you is Mr. Kildare?" he asked, bowing a little.

Kildare hesitated and the man went on. "If so, I would like to speak with you quickly—in private. It is dangerous for me to be here."

Kildare jerked his head toward the door. "Go in." His right hand was in his pocket now, and there was something protruding ominously from it.

The Chinaman obeyed instantly, walking forward with quick, short steps. Kildare and Hazard followed him into the lobby. Kildare stopped suddenly, stood stock still when—

"John," he shouted to the doorman, "close the door!"

Hazard stared in bewilderment.

"What is it?" he demanded.

Kildare looked puzzled.

"I don't know. It seemed to me that I felt something going by. Do you remember as a youngster hearing a spitball blown through a pipe, just missing you?"

"I—I—"

"Well, that's the way this sounded," Kildare cut in, "only not as loud."

As he spoke, the heavy glass grating swung shut. The Chinaman looked bewildered, too.

"What was it?" he asked.

"Something went by," Kildare told him. "I don't know what it was, but I've got a pretty good hunch. Wait."

He stepped back into the lobby and looked out toward the heavy glass door at the front of the building. Turning his head slowly, he glanced from the door to the spot where he had been standing when he had heard the noise. Then he took Hazard by the arm and placed him on the spot.

"Stay here a minute," he said.

Hazard obeyed, but his mind was a fog of bewilderment. He saw Kildare step to the front door and speak to the doorman.

"Where were you standing right after we entered? You were to my right, weren't you?"

"Yes, sir."

"Did you hear anything that sounded like—" Kildare made a slight clucking sound with his tongue, and blew the air from between his lips.

The doorman thought for a moment. "You mean just after you entered?"

"Yes."

"Come to think about it, I believe I heard something of the kind."

"I heard it very plainly," said Kildare, "but that was because the missile passed very close to my head. And you"—he turned to the Chinaman—"did you hear anything pass close by you?"

THE CHINAMAN'S face was sober now. "Perhaps. It seems I was aware of something like a small object flying close to my face, although I couldn't be sure of it, Mr. Kildare."

"All right," Kildare said. "Now let's see. It passed right by my left ear where you're standing, Jerry. It missed me and swished past the face of our Chinese friend before the elevator."

Kildare walked toward a heavy drape that partially screened a sitting room in the rear of the lobby. Instinctively, Hazard followed him.

"You think a poison insect was hurled in after us, I suppose," Hazard ventured.

Kildare shook his head. "No, it didn't seem quite like that to me."

Hazard's eye caught something concealed in the heavy drape—a tiny splinter of wood, perfectly round on one side and square on the back.

"Look! What's this, Kildare?" he asked.

Kildare knocked Hazard's hand away.

"Don't touch it," the government man warned. "I see it now. That's it."

He took his handkerchief and gingerly drew a small, wooden dart from the portière. It was no larger than a loud-toned phonograph needle, but was formed of a fiber substance instead of steel.

"May I ask what it is, Mr. Kildare?" asked the Chinese.

"You may," said Kildare. "It's a poison dart and it was meant, I believe, to kill either you or me."

The bland face of the yellow man never changed. "I was afraid of that," he said, "but I believe I have done right in coming here, nevertheless. I am still alive and I have some important things to tell you."

"You didn't know you were followed here, did you?" Kildare asked.

"No, I didn't."

Kildare jerked his head toward the elevator. "Let's go up to my apartment at once."

KILDARE'S SMALL apartment was located on the seventeenth floor. As he turned his key in the lock, Hazard stood close behind him, gun in hand, ready for instant action. But nothing happened. The door swung open easily. Kildare switched on the lights and led the way into the living room. Somewhere off in the night a clock struck three.

"I think we're safe here," he said. "These windows overlook the river; the roof of the closest building is eight stories below.

It is impossible for anyone to spy on us. But I think it best to get underway as soon as possible."

He addressed this remark to the Chinese, who bowed politely. Kildare motioned him to a chair, took out a box of cigars and passed them.

"Now," he said, settling down in a chair, and winding one long leg around the other, "who are you and why have you taken the chance of coming here?"

"I am Doctor Liang," the Chinese explained.

Kildare's eyes widened. "I am glad to know you, doctor," he said warmly. "I have heard about you."

"Thank you," said the doctor. "I have as one of my patients a Mr. Wu in Chinatown."

Kildare jerked upright.

"You don't mean Wu Fang, do you?"

"I believe that is his full name," said the other calmly. "I also believe that he is going to leave on a trip to Peru very shortly." "HE TOLD you so himself?" Kildare said eagerly. "It's mighty good of you to chance coming here, Doctor Liang."

"That," said the doctor, "is not my main reason for doing it. I had suspicions, of course, as to whom my patient really was, but"—he smiled—"it's part of a doctor's job to keep his patients' secrets. I have treated Mr. Wu for some serious burns. Tonight there was revealed to me one of the most marvelous cures I have ever seen."

Hazard and Kildare listened intently while he described the contents of the earthen jar and its action upon burned and blistered flesh.

"I asked Mr. Wu for the formula of this healing salve," Doctor Liang went on, "but he only laughed and said that perhaps someday he might have to use it as a ransom. I presume he meant either to get himself out of trouble or to raise money, if that time should ever come. I am here in the interests of the medical profession."

"You mean," demanded Kildare, "that you're going to tell us where Wu Fang can be found so that we'll capture him and thereby learn the formula?"

"Precisely," nodded Doctor Liang. "And now I will tell you where you will find Wu Fang. He occupies a series of separate chambers three stories underground in Chinatown. The entrance is off a passage at number sixteen Pell Street. If you will go there, you will find a tea shop in the front of the building. There is a steep stairway leading from the street at the side of the shop. Follow that into a basement below. At the rear of the basement, you will find a trapdoor and below that, another flight that will take you into an underground corridor. At the end of that corridor, a door blocks the passage. You will knock three times, and if you have the same good fortune that I have had, the door will be opened immediately."

Jerry Hazard was growing more rigid in his chair as he listened to Doctor Liang's words.

"But do you think he is still there?" Kildare asked the doctor.

"It is very possible," said Doctor Liang, "since it would take some time for the beautiful young woman who is nursing him to treat his burns."

Hazard leaned forward. "The beautiful young woman? What did she look like?"

Doctor Liang turned slowly. "She was dark and quite tall. I remember her eyes; they held a sort of haunting look."

"Do you know what he called her?" Hazard asked tensely. "Was it Mohra?"

"That was it." The doctor nodded.

"And you say she has been nursing him ever since you've been going there?"

"She has nursed him on each of my visits, but until tonight Mr. Wu has not been fully conscious."

"I knew there was an explanation for it," Kildare cut in. "Wu Fang was burned badly and hasn't been himself since the night of the fire. He's had his agents watching us constantly, but he hasn't given them any orders about doing away with us until tonight."

Hazard was listening only vaguely. His mind was still on Mohra.

"Then she's all right?" he asked the doctor. "She's not burned or disfigured?"

"There were a few slight burns on her arms and legs," the doctor told him, "but her face—I presume you are most interested in that—was not touched by the fire."

Hazard sank back in the chair with a sigh of relief.

"But look here," Kildare probed, "you say—"

He never finished the sentence. He leaped from his chair, eyes fixed on the window behind the Chinese doctor. The shade was up and a dim light gleamed in; but this illumination was partially blotted by a strange form. He saw a hideous yellow hairy face and a squat, shrunken, half-naked body with short, stubby arms and long legs like those of a monkey.

There was a crash as the figure slammed through the window. Between the hideous lips was a straight, narrow pipe about eighteen inches long. Suddenly, the creature blew on the pipe.

A tiny object flashed through the broken window with lightning-like speed, straight for Doctor Liang's neck. The doctor stiffened; with a jerk his mouth opened, and his eyes dilated horribly. As Hazard and Kildare leaped past him, his body went limp and sank with a thud to the floor.

CHAPTER 5
THE APE-MAN

KILDARE STRUGGLED to get his automatic, but somehow his muscles would not respond. The ghastly, eerie figure at the window vanished suddenly.

"What is it?" Hazard gasped.

He hurled the broken window sash upward and stared out into the night. Hazard had his gun free now and leaned out beside him. They stared into the blackness but could see nothing. The form that had been there a second before had vanished as if at the command of a master magician.

After a moment, Kildare said, "I saw it, but I can't believe it. We must be dreaming."

"Where—where could it have gone?" Hazard stammered.

Kildare shook his head, helplessly. "I'll be damned if I know," he admitted. "The creature seemed to drift off into space. Wait! I'll get my electric torch and we'll see if we can spot it. If it leaped from the windowsill, it's dead by now."

He stalked over to his desk and returned in an instant, flashlight in hand.

"You mean it might have tried to jump to the roof below?" Hazard asked.

"Yes. But there's nothing that could make that jump but a cat! It's eight stories down—that's seventy feet at least."

The beam was turned on the roof below. It was entirely empty. The two men stared at each other, speechless. Finally Kildare turned away, the most baffled expression on his face that Hazard had ever seen.

He bent over Doctor Liang's body, where it lay in a crumpled heap. With his thumbs, he spread the skin around the tiny puncture in the fleshy part of the neck.

"Hell!" he exclaimed. "That stuff must be powerful." Then he rose and shrugged. He picked up his cigar from the stand and re-lighted it; then loaded his automatic and sat down, his gun ready for action.

"Sit down and keep an eye on that window while I make a few phone calls," he said.

"A few calls?" Hazard asked. "You're certainly not going to call a physician, are you?"

"No, but I'm going to call the coroner."

He reached for the phone, called the coroner, and made his report. Then he called John, the doorman.

"Have you seen any strange, hairy man that looked like a half-monkey around the building?" he asked.

An exclamation of horror came to him.

"Oh, I don't think there's anything for you to be alarmed about, John," he hurried on. "The main thing I wanted to report was a broken window. Will you see that it's attended to in the morning?"

He hung up the receiver and looked ruefully at his burned clothing.

"Don't forget, Jerry," he said, "to keep an eye on that window. I'm going to change my clothes. Then, we'll take a trip to Chinatown. The coroner should be here any minute."

The government man went into his bedroom and began stripping off the ruined suit. A few minutes later, he returned, fully clothed, with a sheet of paper in his hand.

"This," he said, "is what Captain Falstaff had almost finished deciphering when Mrs. Beemer screamed for help."

He handed the message to Hazard. The newspaperman took the paper and scanned the words. Under each of the queer syllables, Falstaff had written the English equivalent.

I BELIEVE I HAVE LOCATED THE YELLOW MASK OF UNGA. HAVE IMPORTANT INFORMATION CON-CERNING ITS POWER. A MAP WHICH I FOUND ON A TEMPLE WALL SHOWS THE MASK'S HIDING PLACE. UNGA RULED LONG BEFORE THE INCAS CAME TO PERU. HIS DOMAIN WAS SPREADING IN EVERY DIRECTION WITH THE AID OF HIS YELLOW

MASK. THERE IS A STRANGE POWER RECEIVED FROM THIS MASK THAT NO ONE CAN EXPLAIN. IF WE CAN SECURE THIS MASK AND LEARN THE SECRET, IT WILL MAKE YOUR DOMINATION SIMPLE. I AM IN PERU NOW AND WILL AWAIT YOUR ORDERS. WE MAY HAVE TROUBLE WITH THE PRESIDENT OF PERU BUT HE WILL BE TAKEN CARE OF—

JERRY HAZARD was possessed of a queer, unnatural feeling that he could not explain. He looked up with a frown of perplexity.

"What does it all mean?" he demanded.

"I have heard something of it before," Kildare said. "Unga was one of the most powerful rulers in the history of Peru. He used this golden mask to further his influence; at least, that seems to be the legend. Anyway, I think we can be sure of one thing. Wu Fang is going to have a tough time getting out of this country. I've blocked every possible means of escape. Naturally, he'll want to get to Peru as quickly as possible; and that means he'll go by air. Let's see what we can learn from the various airports."

He called Floyd Bennett Field and asked several questions. When he hung up a slight smile of satisfaction was on his face.

"There's something there," he said. Wu Fang or one of his agents tried to charter a plane to fly them out of the country without passports. Now let's see what Roosevelt Field has to say."

Again he asked the same questions. He hung up the phone and shrugged.

"I guess that fixes it," he said. "Apparently, Wu Fang hasn't had much luck in getting out of the country since I warned the airports."

The government man fell silent. His eyes narrowed thoughtfully.

"You know, Jerry," he said, "it's a funny thing Wu Fang doesn't have an airplane of his own."

"There's no telling," Hazard said, "why Chinamen do or don't do certain things."

"Right," said Kildare, "and the more I see and hear of Wu Fang, the more I realize the truth of that remark."

"Well, I don't think we need to worry about his having escaped in a plane," Hazard remarked. "We've got him pretty well bottled up."

"Yes," Kildare admitted, "but it isn't like him to let a thing like that bother him."

"Do you think he'll get through to Peru?"

"He may," Kildare admitted. "I haven't any doubt that he'll try. I suppose it seems funny to be so anxious to get rid of Wu Fang and still block his chances of getting out of the country. We've got to do it, though, to catch him. And I think we're going to come closer to doing it this time than we ever have before."

"I wouldn't like anything better than to be able to catch that yellow devil and finish him off," Hazard said, "provided of course—"

"Yes, I know," Kildare said with a smile, "provided Mohra isn't harmed. I feel mighty sorry for her. I'm quite sure now that she doesn't want to help Wu Fang any more than we want to, but there's always a question as to how much thinking she does for herself."

"Just what do you mean?" Hazard demanded.

The creature blew on the pipe; a tiny object flashed from it.

"It ought to be apparent to you, Jerry. At first, I thought she was a willing slave of Wu Fang—scheming female who was working with him. With the idea of course, that when he dominated the world, she would be his queen. But I've changed my mind. Wu Fang seems to have some spell over her. That's another one of the things we'll find out some day. And as for this yellow mask of Unga—"

Hazard looked at him sharply. "Good Lord!" he exclaimed. "You don't believe the stuff you were telling me about that mask do you?"

Kildare leaned forward. "Jerry, I never believe anything until I see it, but I do know this: Wu Fang never goes after something that isn't damn important. That's what makes me afraid there's something in all this. From indications, he's really trying to get hold of it, and unless we do a better job than we have up till now, he's going to get to Peru. If he succeeds, it's going to be just too bad."

A knock sounded on the door. Kildare walked to the door, and opened it with a quick movement. A paunchy, rather jolly individual looked in.

"Oh, hello, coroner," Kildare said. "We've been waiting for you. You got my report?"

"I got a report that somebody had been killed in your apartment." The coroner chuckled. "But they didn't tell me who it was." He grinned more broadly as he continued, "I rather hoped it was you, Kildare. If you got bumped off, it would make less work for me. Here I was safely in bed for the night, and then I get called out at this ungodly hour of the morning."

"Well, really," Kildare said, smiling, "I'm sorry to have annoyed you, coroner, but work is work, you know. I think when we get Wu Fang your troubles will be over."

The coroner laughed. "I'm just waiting patiently. It won't be long, Val, before I'll be carrying you out."

"I wish you a lot of rotten luck!" Kildare laughed. "You know Jerry Hazard?"

"Sure," said the coroner. "Is he still alive too?"

"I hope to tell you," Hazard assured him, "and what's more, I'm going to stay alive."

THE CORONER poked the body of Doctor Liang with the toe of his foot.

"Who's this guy and what's the matter with him?"

"He's a Chinese doctor," Kildare said. "Doctor Liang."

The coroner rolled the body over and looked at the face of the dead man.

"Doctor Liang," he said. "He was quite famous. Too bad, too bad. He was really an aid to medical science."

Kildare nodded and pointed to the dart at the back of the neck. The coroner glanced at the window near the body.

"Let's see how good a detective I am," he said. "Somebody climbed up this building from a roof just below, kicked in a window, and blew a poison dart at the doctor."

"You aren't far wrong," Kildare said, "except for the fact that it's eight stories to the roof below. Look for yourself."

"No, thanks," said the coroner. "I'll take your word for it. There might be another dart in that gun. But how did the guy get up this high?"

"He had very long legs," Kildare said. "Long legs and short arms and a hairy face. The building goes straight up for eight stories without any balconies, fire escapes, or anything of that kind to hang onto. It's just a flat brick wall."

"Maybe he had legs eight stories long," the coroner said, chuckling.

"No," said Kildare—he lowered his voice now—"but he had wings. You see, when he left, he floated right off into space. It looked as though he had jumped eight stories, but when we looked down there was no sign of him."

The smile suddenly fled from the jovial face of the coroner. His eyes shifted quickly from Kildare to the broken window.

"That's enough for me," he said with a quick nod. "When angels start flying around and kicking in windows with their bare feet and blowing poisonous darts through them, I know one coroner that's going to find a deep, dark hole to hide in."

He waddled quickly to the door and called to the men in the hallway.

"Come in, boys," he said. "You've got a load to lug this time."

Two assistants entered with a long basket. They picked the body of the doctor up and unceremoniously dumped it into the basket. The wicker creaked as they strained at the handles.

The coroner paused at the door, and his chubby face beamed. He waved his hand in casual farewell. "I'll be seeing you on a marble slab."

"Not if I know it, you won't," Kildare laughed back as he closed the door. Then the smile faded from his lips. Grimly he inspected his automatic.

"Now," he said, "we're going to take a little trip to 16 Pell Street. If we run into Wu Fang, let him have it without any argument."

NUMBER 16 Pell Street was exactly as Doctor Liang had

described it. As the cab let them off in front of it, Hazard remarked, "There's the tea shop; and there's the stairway that leads from the sidewalk just as he said."

"But, of course," Kildare reminded him, "it's just like every other entrance in Chinatown. A hole in the sidewalk about three feet square at the front of the building with a little railing on either side of it and a chain stretched across to keep pedestrians from falling in."

As he spoke, he unfastened the chain that hung limp between the rails at the sides of the entrance. Pell Street, except for a drunken white man in evening clothes and a mincing Chinese figure up the street, seemed to be entirely deserted.

Kildare hesitated as the drunk approached them, stumbling and weaving from side to side. He left the chain as it had been before.

The drunk swayed up to them, calling, "Taxshi, taxshi!"

Kildare pointed down the street to the corner of Mott and Pell Streets.

"You might find one there," he said.

The drunk wavered and attempted to bow. "Shanku, shanku very mush."

He was fumbling for something. Finally, he brought out a crumpled pack of cigarettes, selected one with great care, and straightened it out with shaky fingers.

"Could I trouble eisher one of you gen'men for a light?" he asked.

Kildare snapped on his cigar lighter and held it before the

swaying cigarette. The drunk puffed until he got it lighted and then swayed back on his heels.

"Shanku, shanku very mush," he repeated between hiccups. "Well, I've got to toddle along now. I'll be sheeing you."

Kildare and Hazard watched him sway down the street.

"That bird sure has a load on," Hazard observed.

"I wonder," said Kildare with a frown. "If not, he puts on a fine act."

He unfastened the chain again. Suddenly, he stopped and looked down the street.

"Where did that fellow go, Jerry?" he asked. "Did you see him?"

"Who?" Hazard asked. "The drunk?"

"Yes."

Hazard stared toward the corner now. "That's funny," he said. "He's gone, isn't he? He must have turned the corner."

"It's possible," Kildare admitted, "except that when I saw him last, he was swaying along about three doors from the corner."

Suddenly, Kildare dropped the chain and began running down the street.

"Come on," he hissed. He ran in the direction the drunk had taken. Three doors from the corner he stopped and stared down a deep, dark stairway that led underground. Only a dim light was cast by the scattered street lamps. All the buildings were dark except for a meager luminance that shone through torn shades in the house across the street.

The beam of Kildare's electric torch cut the blackness of the stairway. The chain that should have been fastened across the front of it hung from one of the posts, and the space was open.

"Do you suppose that bird fell down here?" Hazard demanded.

Kildare was already running down the steep steps into the black chamber beneath.

"If he did," he answered, "he isn't here now."

CHAPTER 6
16 PELL STREET

JERRY HAZARD plunged after the government man and switched on his electric torch. There was a little areaway about four feet square at the bottom of the stairs. But there was no sign of the drunk, nothing except a door that stood partly ajar.

Something squealed almost directly beneath Hazard's feet. He jumped as though he had been shot and leaped to one side. His head brushed against cobwebs and he fought them off frantically.

Kildare stepped back before the door, kicked it wide open with his foot. More squeals came and something ran over Hazard's instep. He gasped and kicked at it blindly.

"What is it?" Kildare demanded.

"Rats," Hazard shot back, shuddering with distaste.

"Oh," said Kildare, relieved. "If that's all we encounter, we'll be lucky. Come on."

The beam of his light penetrated the inky blackness beyond

the gaping door, revealing an empty room. As they filed in through the narrow entrance, a musty odor greeted them—the smell of an enclosure that had not been opened to the sun and air for a long period of time. There was a chill and dampness that seemed to clasp Hazard in a clammy embrace. Except for the sound of the squealing rats, the place seemed quite still. They played the beams of their lights about the walls.

Hazard kicked viciously at the rats, and a loud curse exploded uncontrollably from his lips.

"Sssh," Kildare warned, "there's no need in letting all Chinatown know we're here."

Again there was complete silence.

"Something queer here," Kildare said. "I don't like the feel of it."

The words sent a chill through Hazard. He stammered, "Wh-whatisit?"

"That drunk came down these stairs, I'm sure of it. And he came down in a mighty big hurry, too."

"Meaning, of course," Hazard said, "that he wasn't as drunk as he appeared to be."

"Exactly. He came down the same way we did."

"Yes," Hazard admitted, "but where could he have gone from here?"

"You tell me," Kildare said, "and I'll see that you get a medal for good work. So far as I can see, there isn't a single way he could have gotten—"

He jumped suddenly and kicked viciously at something that raced across the floor.

"Confound these rats!"

"Why are you so sure he came down here?" Hazard asked.

"Because the last time I saw him, he was swaying toward this stairway. Then my attention was taken away from him for a split second. When I looked again, he was gone. He couldn't have gone anywhere except down these stairs."

Hazard felt a tightening in his throat as he tried to speak again.

"But look here," he said, "isn't it rather ridiculous to talk about that drunk coming down here? When the room has no outlet and he isn't here, anywhere?"

"You mean," Kildare corrected, "into a room that apparently has no outlet. Come on. I'll take this side of the room and you take the other. We'll look over every board and beam; there must be some trick door that will let us out of here."

The work that Kildare had outlined wasn't much to Hazard's liking, although he followed orders. He had his gun in his hand and as he encountered rats, he struck at them. It took but a few minutes to make a complete search of the little room. Its measurements didn't exceed ten feet square.

Hazard had almost given up hope. He had scoured his side, but the search was futile. He was about to ask Kildare what luck he had had when he heard a sound behind him that made his scalp tingle. It seemed to drift down the stairway and it reached them very faintly. Almost instantly, there was another sound, more ominous. It was a muffled boom.

HAZARD STARTED violently as he heard it. Then spun around instantly and swung his light so that it fell full on Kildare.

"Good Lord!" he exclaimed. "What was that?"

Kildare didn't answer. He was lunging toward the door, and then Jerry Hazard understood what that sound had been. The door, the only apparent entrance to this underworld tomb, had closed, as though a phantom hand had moved it. Both men focused their lights on the portal.

"Come on," Hazard shouted, "we've got to break it down. They've got us cornered in here."

But as he stepped back to lunge, Kildare held out his hand.

"Wait," he said in a soft voice.

The beam of his torch shone on the lock.

"I think it was just an accident," he said. "This is a patent lock."

He turned the knob back and forth; suddenly it clicked, and the door opened. Hazard stared in astonishment.

"You mean that nobody pulled that door shut and locked it?"

"Maybe," Kildare said. "I'd expect anything in Chinatown. But it looks to me as though it swung shut by itself. Well, I don't think there's any sense in staying here any longer. The drunk couldn't have gotten in here and left again except by some secret passage, and we haven't been successful in finding it."

"You think the drunk is connected with Wu Fang?" Hazard asked.

"Search me," Kildare said. "You know as much about it as I do. But if he isn't, there's more than one funny thing going on in Chinatown tonight. Come on, we'll go back to 16 Pell Street."

The air in the narrow Chinatown street was fresh and welcomed Jerry Hazard as he hurried up the stairs to the sidewalk. A feeling of thanksgiving welled up within him, and a hope was born that if there were any breaks to be handed out now, perhaps he and Mohra might get their share. His thoughts of the girl were quickly replaced by others as they approached 16 Pell Street.

They stopped before the stairway. Kildare stepped into a shadowy doorway at the side, drew Hazard with him.

"Don't make a move," he whispered. "Watch over there. No, next door. See it? There's something crouched between those buildings. It looked to me as though it were moving on all fours."

Hazard stared and saw something move in the narrow passageway between the buildings.

"Yes," he hissed, "I see it."

He watched steadily for a full half-minute. Then the night swallowed up the creature they were watching.

"What was it?" Hazard asked curiously.

"I don't know," Kildare answered. "Whatever it was, it's gone now. It might have been a dog, but somehow I have a feeling that it was—" He shrugged. "No matter. Let's move on."

Hazard followed him to the sidewalk, but he kept his eyes on that narrow passage across the street. Kildare hesitated before the stairway at the side of the tea shop and slipped his automatic into his left hand as he unlocked the chain guarding the steep steps.

"All right, come on," he whispered. "We're in for it now."

The steps were exactly like the others; they were very narrow, and the hole below into which their flashlight beams penetrated was as dark as an ink bottle.

Hazard counted the steps as they descended. Ten, eleven, twelve, thirteen. That wasn't so good. He tried to tell himself that he wasn't superstitious, only careful.

They came upon a closed door, as they had before. It opened easily, almost too easily, Hazard thought. They passed into a room that apparently had only one entrance.

THE BEAMS from their electric torches played against the walls and across the floor of half-rotted planking. Their tread was hollow, indicating many stories of underground rooms and passages beneath them. Of one thing Hazard was glad. There seemed to be no rats in this place. At least if there were, they were keeping to themselves.

Kildare was searching the floor. "Here it is," he called out softly. "Just as Doctor Liang said it would be."

Hazard hurried over, bent down beside him. There was a heavy trapdoor in the floor. They raised it quietly and turned their flashlight beams down into the dungeonlike pit beneath, into which steps descended. Hazard guessed there must be at least twenty of those steps. They were of stone, and—he found when he trod them a moment later—were slippery and slimy with moisture. They descended cautiously until they reached the bottom.

"Twenty-four steps," Hazard whispered. "I counted them coming down."

"We're a long way underground," Kildare said, "but not nearly as far as we're going before we get through with this."

"I was just thinking," said Hazard as they paused at the bottom of the stairs, "that someday we're going to get advance information on this fellow Wu Fang and then we're going to be ready for him in one of these passages."

"Let's hope so," Kildare said.

Their light beams cut the darkness. For Hazard the corridor was full of dread; although there wasn't a sound, strange odors mingled there, each telling its own story. His nostrils caught the scent of mold. Here and there on the walls, clung fungus. A strange scent of incense filled the air. There came another odor of decayed and rotted flesh.

The passage was too narrow for them to walk abreast. Hazard followed Kildare down the corridor, and their steps, no matter how gently they trod, echoed against the slimy stone walls.

They had gone perhaps fifty feet when Kildare stopped abruptly.

"Ssh!" he breathed. "Listen!"

At first the newspaperman heard nothing. Then a sound came to him, faintly. It was weak, and yet, peculiarly distinct.

Pad! Pad! Pad!

"Did you get it?" Kildare whispered.

"Yes," nodded Hazard in a hollow whisper. "Where does it come from?"

Kildare shrugged. "Damned if I know," he said, "but I think it's over our head."

"It sounded like the quick, shuffling step of a Chinaman."

As they pushed on down the passage their light beams picked out another door which, Hazard guessed, must be at least a hundred feet long. It opened easily and showed them another flight of steps, steep and narrow.

They proceeded carefully, and found themselves in a small underground chamber about six feet square, opening out on another passage. Kildare flashed his light.

"I wonder," he said, in a low voice, "whether those footsteps we heard were over us or down here. This passage looks to me as if it runs directly under the one we just came through."

Instantly, Hazard realized the significance of the statement. If that were true, a yellow man was down here ahead of them. Perhaps he was preparing an unwelcome reception for them.

Hazard voiced this to Kildare, who only shrugged and began to tiptoe down the narrow corridor. Their flashlight batteries had weakened and the light was becoming dimmer, flashing but ten feet ahead.

"It might be a good idea," Kildare whispered, "if you save your light. I think that drunk we saw has done his work well. I'll use up my light and then you can use yours, if necessary."

"Right," Hazard said. He snapped off his torch.

"Suppose you stay about ten feet behind me, Jerry," Kildare suggested, "and keep your gun ready. There's no need of us both getting caught in the same trap."

Again Hazard obeyed and stood still while Kildare passed down the corridor ten feet ahead of him. He followed slowly. Suddenly the door through which they had entered slammed shut.

At the same time, Kildare's light went out, plunging them into utter darkness. Instantly, Hazard rushed forward. He heard a low cry and the sound of scuffling feet. He snapped on his torch and directed the beam down the narrow passage. The corridor was empty. Val Kildare was nowhere in sight.

CHAPTER 7
TOMB OF RATS

"**K**ILDARE! KILDARE!" Hazard yelled frantically. No answer returned to him. He ran to the spot where he had last seen Kildare. There was no trace of him; nor of any door through which he might have vanished. He had simply, unaccountably, disappeared from sight.

Now Jerry Hazard became calm, not because he was unafraid, but with the realization that in moments like these men went mad. His only hope was in calm, sure action and decision. His electric torch battery was nearly exhausted. He ran through the corridor hoping to find some solution to his friend's disappearance.

Twenty feet ahead, a door blocked the narrow passage. He reached it and fumbled frantically for the latch. The door opened. A mass of horrible little beasts rushed over him madly. The room was filled with rats that swarmed over him in a wild, savage rush.

Hazard leaped back and slammed the door shut. He kicked viciously at the rats that had escaped their prison and beat them off in desperation. He felt one climbing up his back; felt the filthy creature's claws through his clothing. Another was crawling up his right leg. They moved with lightning speed, these beasts. Then the flashlight went out, as he struck at a rat, and he could only fight back by feeling his way. Kicking, panting, striking, he fought on. The little beasts climbed over him, ripping spitefully, here and there.

His elbow struck a sharp projection on the stone well, and for a moment his right arm was paralyzed. He continued striking and knocking with the flashlight in his other hand. Another rat leaped onto his back. He whirled and slammed against the wall of the corridor, heard the rodent squeal as he crushed it, then felt it drop from his body and fall soddenly to the floor. The rats persisted in their attack.

It seemed to Hazard, as he continued striking at the rats, that the battle would go on and on until either the rats gnawed a vital place in his body or he dropped from exhaustion.

In these moments of terrific struggle, Jerry Hazard had been alone; and it did something to him. Until now, he had been largely dependent upon Kildare. Now, he was on his own and it had transformed him, by necessity, into a wild, fighting demon. He struck with his gun hand at another rodent that leaped on him; heard the metal crack against its skull. Then he turned defiantly and stared through the inky blackness.

"All right, you damned rats," he rasped out, "come and get it. I'll give you all you're looking for."

For an instant he was lost, unable to decide his next move. He heard a sound behind him; a soft padding of running feet.

He spun around to fire his automatic into the darkness. It might be Kildare, though. He couldn't take the chance.

"Kildare!" he called out. "Is that you?"

Strong arms grasped his legs and a heavy body was thrown against his. He was going down and couldn't seem to help himself. He clutched madly to save himself; and as he fell, he called again, "Kildare!"

The howl of a savage beast came from the creature that tackled him. He raised his gun at his attacker but something struck his arm. As it went numb, he pulled the trigger, the jerk finishing the motion. Flames spurted from the automatic, and, for an instant, illuminated the interior of the narrow passageway. In the light Hazard saw a hideous, brown face, contorted with pain. The bullet had made a hole in the front of the flat nose. Hazard felt the body slump down, and he struggled frantically to get free. The body rolled over away from him and he heard the skull strike the heavy plank floor with a dull thud.

A million thoughts raced through his brain. Kildare was gone and must be saved. His light was out and he couldn't see. He must run and get help. That was the only thing that would come to his mind, the only possible solution. Unless Kildare was dead, already.

Suddenly, something struck him on the shoulder. His right arm had been almost paralyzed by the other blow, but now, all feeling left it. He tried desperately to hold the automatic in his fingers, but it was no use. He heard the gun clatter to the floor as a heavy body slammed him against the side of the corridor, pinioning his left arm behind him.

HAZARD STRUGGLED and fought like a madman, but this creature possessed power with which he couldn't cope. A shout rang out through the corridor from lips that were close to his face. The breath of the yellow man came to his nostrils. It reeked of decayed teeth and sickened him.

Hazard moved the numb fingers of his right hand. That arm wasn't pinioned. Still, it was useless to him.

He heard running feet coming nearer. His captor shouted through the corridor in his singsong Chinese, probably for help. His face was in front of Hazard now, a beautiful target for a right to the jaw, if he could only get that right fist in action. Hazard doubled his fist, as some feeling came back to his fingers, and drew back.

The sound of those running feet approaching, and the knowledge that he was cut off, assisted his strength. Suddenly, he let the punch go, full in the face of the other. It was strong enough, thankfully, to release him.

Hazard stepped back a pace. Both arms were free now, and he measured with his left. This time, as he struck, he heard the yellow devil grunt, and fall to the plank floor. Hazard turned to run away from the sound of advancing feet. Suddenly he realized that he was trapped. He would have to fight his way clear. Behind him was the door that led into the tomb of the starving rats. Down the corridor, before him, came the feet, almost upon him now.

There was only one thing to do and he did that quickly. He bent down with his head lowered, like a football player charging the line. He lunged headlong with his arms outstretched and his shoulders hunched to take the blows. He struck the first man, full in the stomach with his head. A blow on the head left Hazard dazed, but he plunged on. He felt wild hands groping for his flying legs, but he managed to kick free. He struck the next comer, and now his fists were flailing away. He sent the figure reeling against the side of the corridor. He lunged on. Another stood in his way. His right hand shot out. Then something caught his foot. He kicked with all his might and his foot came down on the face of his last assailant. That seemed to make no difference to the hand that clutched his ankle. He was suddenly jerked back by gigantic force, sinking to his knees with a loud crack as they struck the plank floor.

Then suddenly blows were being rained upon his entire body. Fists were flying, Chinamen were screeching, and his body was weighted down by the half-naked forms that were everywhere at once. His head reeled with the blow that struck him in the temple. His arms and legs were pinioned and he was lifted up and carried down the corridor. His head was spinning, but he was aware of a door being opened somewhere along the corridor. A door, or perhaps just the side of the passage, where it was lined with planking.

It was still pitch dark. Presently, he heard another door open. They were going into an inner room now, lighted with a weird, unnatural illumination.

Hazard looked about at his captors now and saw there were five of them. Two of them were brown-skinned, like other Wu Fang agents. The others were Chinese of the coolie type.

His head rang and stars appeared before him as they turned

71

him over. They dropped him unceremoniously on his face, still holding his arms and legs so that he couldn't move. His arms were pinned to his back and his wrists were bound. They picked him up again and set him in a chair. A horrible, flat-nosed Chinaman spoke to him in good English.

"You are Mr. Hazard?" He paused for an instant and then went on, "You need not answer. We know already. You have come to find the hiding place of Wu Fang." His face contorted with a hideous grin. "Do you know what will happen to you?"

He glared savagely at Hazard, who simply stared back silently. He strained at the thongs that bound his wrists. It was no use. Those fellows had done a good job when they bound him.

The yellow devil repeated what he had just said, but still Hazard didn't answer. The heavy shoulders shrugged.

"It doesn't matter," the Chinaman said, "I will tell you. You are about to be offered in sacrifice to Chang Li, our God of the Lost Souls."

A shiver of apprehension passed through Hazard. "Chang Li? Who is he?"

The other bowed at the mention of the name.

"You wouldn't understand," he said. "I have already told you Chang Li is our God of the Lost Souls. That is sufficient for us; to you it need not matter. You are one of the arch enemies of Chang Li. Therefore, you will be a most fitting sacrifice, Mr. Hazard. You will please Chang Li so that he will gratify the desires of our master, Wu Fang."

HAZARD SAT there like a statue, glaring back at him. The Chinaman turned to the others in the room.

"Prepare him for the sacrifice of rats," he ordered.

Rats! The word struck a ghastly note on Hazard's tortured nerves. Good Lord, what were they going to do to him? Throw him to those starving rats as a sacrifice to this God they called Chang Li?

In answer to the command, the brown men turned and vanished behind a heavy drapery. In less than a minute they reappeared, bearing between them a glazed pottery vase. They bowed low and presented it to the squat headman. One of them stepped to the side of the room and threw back another drape, disclosing a grotesque idol wrought in some black medium that resembled ebony.

The Chinaman bore the vase in front of the idol, bowed down on his knees before it. Holding the vase above his head, he began chanting in Chinese. Hazard caught the name Chang Li. So this was the idol of the God of Lost Souls.

The others bowed as the ceremony continued. The headman rose very slowly. A muffled gong sounded. With great deliberation, the Chinaman walked over and stopped before Hazard. Without a word from him, his brown-skinned attendants came forward and took hold of the handles of the vase.

The Chinaman was removing an earthen plug from the top of the vase. He held his hands cupped before the vase, and the attendants poured the liquid on them.

"You will now be anointed for the sacrifice, Mr. Hazard," he sang out.

Hazard was trying to be calm, but it taxed every vestige of self control that he possessed. He couldn't help flinching as the great hands of the Chinaman came up with the liquid. Those hands were touching Hazard's face, rubbing over the skin, caressing it.

Again, the Chinaman turned, and more of the liquid was poured on his hands. This he rubbed on Hazard's hands.

When the process was finished, the yellow devil stepped back with the same maddening leisure. He walked over beside the idol again and chanted in Chinese.

Hazard's flesh crawled. In his half-mad brain, he could feel those hunger-starved rats clawing at him, fighting over bits of his body, gnawing and tearing at him.

The yellow man had turned away from the idol, nodding to the two brown attendants.

"We are ready for the sacrifice," he announced.

The brown men moved toward Hazard in a most reverent fashion. They bent down, one on either side of him, and picked him up. The yellow lord of sacrifice walked before them as they bore Hazard to the other end of the room.

Beyond the Chinaman, Hazard could see a large, silken, embroidered drape on the wall. The headman took hold of one corner and drew it back, disclosing a door in the paneled wall, perhaps two feet square, standing at least four feet above the floor. He was opening the door and they were carrying Hazard toward it. Hazard heard sounds that all but made him scream in terror. It was the scurrying and squealing of the rats beyond that opening.

Then his nerves snapped completely. His wrists and ankles were bound, but he could still move his body. He jerked convulsively, writhed and kicked with all his might. He reverted to a wild, fighting beast. The beginning of a horrible death was but a few seconds away.

The brown, savage fingers that held him began pressing into his arms and shoulders and legs; they found paralyzing nerve centers and worked on them. Hazard realized that his efforts were futile because he was numb in every muscle of his body. They had him in their power and could do as they liked.

He yelled insane threats. The din of the squealing, fighting rats in the death chamber was growing louder as they moved toward it. They were going to plunge him into the tomb of rats, feet first. In fact, his feet were there already and they were moving him forward at a maddeningly slow pace. Hazard made one last, desperate attempt to break away that was futile.

CHAPTER 8
EYES OF THE BLIND

A FEW times during the life of Jerry Hazard, all of his past had flashed before him; but never so vividly as now. Most horrible in his mind, as his end came near, was the thought of the beautiful, dark girl—Mohra. If he were sacrificed, what would become of her? That thought made him forget his own immediate danger, for the instant. The knowledge that she might eventually become the mistress or even the wife of Wu

Fang tortured him insanely. He could see her lovely, exotic face, as his feet were about to be shoved into the small opening.

The rats on the other side of the wall squealed louder. He could hear them leaping up in an effort to get at his feet. Their claws scratched the wall as they struggled to climb to a vantage point—to be ready to pounce upon his body and gnaw it to bits. To gorge themselves on his flesh until there would be nothing left but his bones.

Hazard was struggling desperately, praying that the strength would come back to his muscles. The cruel fingers of the brown men continued to press into the vital nerve centers of his arms and legs. Two, three seconds, perhaps were left to him before his body would plunge into that room beyond, and the rats would swarm over him.

Suddenly, there was a change in the demeanor of all in the room. The Chinaman who held open the door tensed and stared toward the other end of the room; then the squat figure moved with lightning speed. He whirled around with a long knife gleaming in his hand. At the same moment, he uttered a cry of warning to the brown men and leaped toward the center of the room.

All these things happened so quickly that Jerry Hazard didn't realize just what was taking place, except that the pressure on his nerve centers had been relaxed. A shot rang out, but he couldn't see who did it or at whom it was directed. The brown men let go of him and leaped away. He felt a piercing shock of pain as his shoulder struck the floor.

A shrill scream of pain filled the corridor, and he saw the

form of the little Chinaman pitch forward. Then he saw something that filled him with hope and relief. Val Kildare was standing at the other end of the room, having just stepped out from behind the drapes that covered the wall. His face was a mask of icy rage. His automatic spurted flame.

Blam! Blam! Blam!

The bellowing of the gun echoed through the underground room with a deafening roar. Shrieks of anger and pain came from Wu Fang's henchmen.

The knots of the rope that bound Hazard's ankles had caught on the opening to the rat tomb, leaving him hanging with the upper part of his body on the floor. He kicked frantically and broke free.

All vision was cut off as the heavy body of a brown man who had been carrying him fell on him. His foul-smelling stomach smothered Hazard's face. He felt a warm fluid gushing over his eyes, nose, and mouth; knew that it was blood, great stifling masses of it.

He heard Kildare call out, "Good Lord, Jerry, are you hurt?"

Hazard tried to reply but the foul blood of the brown man still filled his nostrils.

Finally, he managed to open his mouth. "No, I'm all right."

He felt Kildare dabbing at his eyes and nose, wiping away the blood.

"Well, Jerry," he said, "you look a lot better now."

HE SLASHED at the bindings around Hazard's wrists and ankles and helped him to his feet. Hazard swayed for a moment, unsteadily. Then he turned, caught hold of the high, small door to the rat tomb, and slammed it shut.

"There," he breathed, "I hope that's over."

He surveyed the room. Five forms were lying prostrate. The figure of the squat yellow man still twitched in the last throes of agony. The others were motionless.

"Thank God you're all right, Kildare," Hazard breathed. "I was afraid you were—"

Kildare nodded. "Yes," he said, "I thought I was in for it myself. But I managed to overpower the yellow devil that snatched me through a secret door, and I learned from him something that isn't particularly pleasant. Wu Fang has gone. He didn't seem to know where or how he was going, except that he was heading for Peru. I also found out something else concerning the mask. According to him, Wu Fang is confident that if he can secure this golden yellow mask it will give him the same power that it gave Unga. He expects not only to use it himself but to be able to transmit that power to every yellow devil of the Chinese race who will work with him for supremacy of the earth."

Kildare moved to where the idol of Chang Li stood. A great candle was burning before it. Kildare picked up the taper and walked toward the drape from behind which he had appeared.

"But Kildare," Hazard said, "you know that's impossible. This mask is probably all a fake founded on legend."

Kildare stopped short.

"You know Wu Fang almost as well as I do by now, Jerry," he said, "or at least you ought to. You should realize then that whether the mask works or not, Wu Fang will find a way to use it."

They were passing through a secret door hidden between the draperies. Kildare continued, "We've got to check every method of escape Wu Fang might employ to get out of New York, and when we find the one he chose, we've got to learn his destination. He'll try to work out some means of flight."

The candle flickered weirdly in the passage through which they were moving. The corridor was winding and had a dank, Oriental smell; but Hazard had no fears, now, except that ever-present one for Mohra's safety. His thoughts always went to her when he felt close to death or even when comparatively safe, as he seemed to be now.

They were moving down the winding passage quite swiftly. Kildare apparently was sure of his destination. Obviously, they were moving away from danger. If there were any more of Wu Fang's agents about, they had taken particular pains to remain out of sight.

A draft of air met them from up the corridor, and Kildare had to shield the flame of the candle to keep it from going out.

"I think we strike the main passage just ahead," he said in a low voice. "We ought to be out on the street before long."

As he spoke, the flickering candlelight revealed a great door. A slight push of Kildare's hand, and it opened easily.

"I left it like that when I came in," he said softly. "Now we're in the main passage going back the way we came."

They walked up steep stairs and opened the door into the passage above. Hazard was just behind Kildare as he topped the stairs and pushed the door. He saw Kildare stop stock still and lower his hand a little before the light.

"Hazard, look!"

Hazard sprang forward. The passageway was too narrow for him to come abreast of Kildare, but he peered over his shoulder at a figure that blocked their way. It was a Chinaman, walking toward them very slowly. He stooped a little as he came, and his steps were not the quick ones of a young Chinaman. Moreover, he seemed to walk with the mechanical motion of a robot.

The light of the candle flickered again and although the figure was a mere half dozen paces ahead of them, it faded into the gloom. Then the flame flared again and they saw him still coming toward them in ghostly fashion, as though he didn't know they were there and wouldn't have cared if he did. On and on he came, step by step.

Suddenly the candle sputtered and went out. For an instant, Hazard tensed like a statue. He fumbled in his pocket for matches. But Kildare beat him to it and was already holding a flame to the candle. As it flared again, Hazard saw that the Chinaman was almost upon them.

"Stop!" Kildare ordered in a low voice. "Stop where you are, or I'll shoot."

The other stopped short and Hazard gasped a little with amazement. The eyes were what held Kildare's and Hazard's attention.

"He's blind, Jerry!"

HAZARD NODDED. He, too, had seen the bleached and staring eyes, as of a man who had been dead for several days.

He couldn't repress a shudder. Not only were the eyeballs ghastly-looking things, but there was matter, thick and yellow, drooling from their corners. The head was nodding slowly in answer to Kildare's mention of his blindness and the shrunken lips moved.

"Yes," the old man said in perfect English, "I am blind. I have been blind many years. My name is Ting Ho. I trust you are the ones I seek, honorable sirs. I heard the shooting and I came, hoping I might carry out the vengeance I have in my heart."

"Whom did you hope to meet?" Kildare asked.

"It is better," said the other, "that we talk in my room. If you will follow, I will lead you there. You may trust me. You are Mr. Kildare?"

"Yes," Kildare answered. "Who was it that you wanted to wreak your vengeance upon?"

"It is not you, I assure you," came the reply. "It is another. Come, you will follow and I will lead the way, honorable sirs."

With that, Ting Ho turned, without waiting for them to reply. Kildare and Hazard followed without further questioning. The old man shuffled up the corridor in the same automatic fashion.

Fifty feet farther on, he stopped short. In the light of the candle, Hazard saw him extend his hand and push against the wall. With a slight creaking of hinges, a door opened into another passage.

"You will close the door, please," the old man said.

The passage ended in a little room scarcely more than eight feet square, from which stairs went up along the opposite wall.

The old man led them up through a trapdoor into a large, orientally furnished living room. Except for the light thrown by the candle, the room was pitch dark.

"You will excuse no light in here, please," the old man said, turning to them. "I have no need of light."

"It's quite all right," Kildare assured him quickly. "We have a light with us."

"I will sit in my chair," said Ting Ho, "and you will please take other seats."

He sank into a heavily carved chair, and Kildare and Hazard dropped onto a low couch. They waited a moment in intense silence. Then the old Chinaman spoke again.

"I had a son," he said, "my only child." His voice was little more than a husky whisper. "He was employed by one known as Wu Fang. My son's work displeased Wu Fang, and he was killed. I have one thing to live for now that my son is dead." He hesitated and the blank eyes stared through the two men. "You are quite sure one of you is Mr. Kildare?"

The government man nodded. "Yes," he said, "I am Kildare, Val Kildare, and this is Jerry Hazard, my assistant."

"I have heard both your names mentioned by Wu Fang through a little device that I have installed in his chamber," Ting Ho went on. "It is well. He has sent his agents to kill you both and he has fled, taking his important agents with him. You may be able to capture him in time if you pursue him immediately. He is going to Peru—by plane. He has chartered a large passenger plane from Newark airport. It is bound for the Pacific coast, but he hopes to overpower the pilots and force them to fly him to Peru."

Hazard was on the edge of his chair. He saw Kildare lean forward and ask, "Did you hear him say all this?"

The old man nodded. "Yes," he said, "I heard it all from his chamber. I have wires from there leading to this room. Do you think you can catch him?"

Kildare leaped to his feet. "We'll certainly do our best," he promised. "Did you hear anything more?"

"Only about the gold mask of an ancient ruler called Unga," the old man said. "No doubt you already know about that."

"Yes," Kildare nodded. "I think we know as much as possible about that, but let's get this trip straight. You say he's chartered one of the passenger planes from Newark airport to fly him and his agents to the Pacific coast? And he plans to force the two pilots to change their course and fly him to Peru? Is that correct?"

"That is correct," Ting Ho assured him. "Unless the pilots are warned it will be quite easy for Wu Fang to do as he plans. The Dragon Lord of Crime stops at nothing."

The old man rose from his chair and moved across the room.

"You will go out this way, honorable sirs," he said. "Just ahead you will find a narrow stairway leading to a trapdoor. You may go into the back of the tea shop through that, to the street."

Ting Ho stepped aside. His hand groped for a little stand at the side of the door. On it stood a small, beautifully wrought Chinese vase.

"And now," he said, "my work is done. I have nothing more to live for. Goodbye."

Hazard saw the hand of the Chinaman grasp the vase. With a movement quicker than he had judged the man capable of, Ting Ho brought it up to his lips.

"Stop him!" Hazard exclaimed in alarm. "He's drinking the stuff in that vase!"

Before Hazard or Kildare could reach Ting Ho, he had tipped the vase up. They saw the gaunt muscles of his throat move as he swallowed. Then the vase crashed to the floor and the old Chinaman slumped down at their feet.

Hazard caught him as he fell, and Kildare was beside him an instant later. Kildare rose, shaking his head pityingly.

"Poor old fellow," he said, "he'll have no more worries from now on."

"Dead?" gasped Hazard.

Kildare nodded and turned toward the door that Ting Ho had opened just before taking the poison.

"Come on," he said, "we've got to get out of here."

His words trailed off as he ran up the narrow stairs, Hazard close upon his heels. A few moments later, they were on the sidewalk at 16 Pell Street.

CHAPTER 9
DANGER SKIES

O N THEIR arrival at the Newark airport, Kildare and Hazard went straight to the executive office of the airport company. The clerk on duty opened his eyes a little wider as he saw the badge of authority displayed by Kildare. He straightened, ready to take any order.

"Sometime during the night," Kildare said, "you sent out a special ship to carry a group of people to the coast. Is that correct?"

The clerk nodded. "Yes, sir," he said.

"Do you know who made the arrangements?"

The clerk hesitated and glanced at the passenger list.

"Yes, sir," he replied. "It was a Mr. Lamacha."

"Can you describe him?"

"I wasn't here at the time," the clerk answered, "but the night man said a whole crowd came down. They seemed to be in a hurry to get to the coast. They had a lot of baggage with them."

"How many were there in the party?" Kildare asked.

Again the clerk consulted the list. "Thirteen."

"That's not so good," Hazard remarked.

"Right," nodded Kildare. "It means bad luck to somebody. May I see the passenger list?"

"Yes, sir." The clerk nodded politely, handing the list to him. There were names there, none of which meant anything to the enemies of Wu Fang. Although Hazard's heart pounded a little faster as he saw the name of a woman, Miss Alcatraz.

"They are all fictitious," Kildare remarked, handing the list back to the clerk, "but that's the outfit, all right."

"The night man told me that a vaudeville troupe had just chartered a separate plane to the coast," the clerk ventured.

Kildare nodded very slowly. "Yes," he said, "I guess that's

pretty close. If they are successful, they'll put on the most damnable show that this old globe ever laid eyes on."

"You want to catch them?" the clerk asked.

"Yes, but first we've got to warn the pilots of that plane. Have you any idea where they are now?"

"Yes, sir, I can tell you in a minute," the clerk nodded. He glanced at the clock on the wall and then to a great map beneath it. "That plane ought to be just a little past Chicago by now," he said.

"Can you reach them on the shortwave radio at that distance?" Kildare asked.

"I'll try," the clerk said. He turned and switched on the set at the other end of the room.

"Let me talk to the pilot if you get him," Kildare instructed.

"Yes, sir," the other said, nodding. "Newark calling 1091. Newark calling 1091. Newark calling Pilot Boggs, 1091. Newark calling 1091."

He repeated the call for two minutes, then he switched off the sending apparatus and tuned in the receiving set. For half a minute nothing happened; then a faint, metallic voice came from the speaker.

"1091 calling Newark. 1091 calling Newark. Boggs, 1091 calling Newark. Go ahead."

The clerk switched on the sending apparatus again and began talking.

"This is Newark," he said. "There's a government man here who wants to talk to you. I'll put him on."

"Go ahead."

Kildare bent down to the microphone. "Listen, Boggs. You've got a dangerous cargo on board. There's thirteen passengers, one of them a woman. Right?"

Boggs' voice came back, "Right. Thirteen of them and one a woman. And boy, is she a honey!"

Hazard felt his muscles tighten, but he made no move. Kildare went on.

"Don't show any sign of surprise at what I'm going to tell you. You're probably being watched very carefully. One of the men you have as a passenger is tall, with narrow shoulders, and pretty well muffled up so you can't see his face, isn't he?"

"Right," came Pilot Boggs' reply. "He's wearing dark glasses, too. Does that tally?"

"Yes," Kildare shot back. "I don't know which one he's supposed to be on the passenger list but his real name is Wu Fang. Perhaps you've heard of him."

There was a slight hesitation before Boggs' reply came, but his voice was quite steady as he said, "Right. I get it. And the rest?"

"They are some of his agents," Kildare told him. "You haven't had any trouble yet, have you?"

"Not the least," the pilot answered.

"You will, though," Kildare said. "When you get down toward the Mexican border, they'll try to overpower you. Be prepared. We'll be following in another plane immediately. Try to fake engine trouble and lay up at Wichita."

Pilot Boggs thought fast. "I get it, chief," he said. "Bad weather ahead. Tie up at Wichita until further orders. Right."

"Right," Kildare sang out.

Several people were in the waiting room. It was time for the big transport whose motors were blasting away outside to be taking off.

Kildare turned and went out of the inner office to where Hazard was waiting for him. He jerked his head toward the roaring monster out on the line in the gray light of early morning.

"Does this plane go over the same route as the one they chartered?" he asked.

"Yes, sir," the clerk nodded.

"Come on, Jerry," Kildare snapped. "We're taking it."

HAZARD DID some fast thinking in the meantime. "Aren't you afraid," he asked as they stepped out of the waiting room into the early morning air, "that someone might have come into the waiting room and heard you?"

"It's possible," Kildare nodded, "but that's one of the chances we will have to take. Too bad this two-way shortwave wireless can't be more of a private phone booth affair."

They walked rapidly to the waiting transport plane and climbed aboard. Kildare turned to Hazard.

"I pity that pilot Boggs," he said. "He's going to have his hands full. I have a hunch from the way he acted that one of Wu Fang's agents was standing at the door between the passenger compartment and the pilot's cabin. You heard him pull that stunt about bad weather beyond Wichita? Clever fellow, that pilot. I think we're going to get somewhere. You take one of the seats back here, and I'll be back in a few minutes. I want to talk to the pilots."

Hazard sat down and waited while Kildare went into the pilots' cockpit. He talked there for perhaps five minutes.

During that time, the cabin was filling with passengers. Hazard checked them as they came in.

A businessman. A young woman, probably a movie star; anyway she was very good looking, he observed. With her was a young man. Other men came in, average American businessmen. A stately, elderly woman with white hair was next. She looked more than sixty but was well preserved. Nine passengers in all, besides themselves, in the big transport.

Suddenly, as the pilots' door opened and Kildare began walking down the aisle, Hazard's attention was drawn outside by a small figure running toward the plane. A lad was coming at top speed with a bunch of papers under one arm and something that looked like an envelope in the other. It was Cappy, and he was yelling at the top of his voice.

"Jerry! Jerry! Where are you?"

The great motors were blasting away savagely. Hazard leaped from his seat.

"Run to the pilots' cockpit and stop the plane," he told Kildare. "Cappy's coming and he's got something for us."

Kildare whirled, ran toward the door he had just left. Hazard turned to the passenger entrance at the rear of the cabin and flung it open as the ship was about to pull away. He heard the roar of the motors cut back.

"Cappy!" he called. "What is it?"

He saw the boy turn eagerly, saw a look of relief cross his face. Then the newsboy ran toward him, still waving the envelope. He came up to the door, leaped to the step. Jerry Hazard helped him inside.

"A funny-looking guy handed me this a little while ago on the corner where I sell papers," he panted breathlessly. "It's for you. I asked them at the office where you were, and they told me you were leaving from Newark airport, so I hurried out here as fast as I could."

Jerry Hazard tore open the letter. He saw Kildare out of the corner of his eye, coming down the aisle. The plane's motors still idled, waiting for the command to go.

"What is it?" Kildare said in a low voice.

"Please let me go, too," Cappy pleaded. "Please let me go with you."

Kildare read the note over Hazard's shoulder. He turned and went forward up the aisle. A moment later, the motors roared out. The ship took off; and Cappy was with them. The lad's face beamed with delight and anticipation, as his wish was fulfilled.

Jerry Hazard's mind was completely engrossed with the letter Cappy had brought. He read it again to make sure of its contents.

DEAR JERRY:

WE ARE GOING AWAY. WU FANG HAS SWORN TO KILL YOU BOTH. PLEASE, PLEASE GO OFF AND HIDE. HE IS DETERMINED TO GET YOU THIS TIME. HE IS LEAVING SOME OF HIS AGENTS ON YOUR TRAIL. ABOVE ALL, DO NOT TRY TO FOLLOW. IF YOU LOVE ME, PLEASE DO AS I ASK.

MOHRA

THE CASE OF THE YELLOW MASK

HAZARD STOOD in a daze. The salutation flashed again and again through his mind. And the last—"If you love me." Mohra must care, too. If not, he argued to himself, why this note—in all probability, at great danger to herself?

Dimly, he felt Cappy tugging his arm and saw the lad grinning delightedly at him.

"Come on, Jerry," he exclaimed. "Gee, you aren't going to stand up all the way to the coast, are you?"

Hazard turned. He seemed to be walking on air. Kildare took a seat beside him, across the aisle, with Cappy just ahead. He looked out the window and saw the Delaware River winding beneath. He heard Kildare's voice close to his ear.

"You aren't planning to follow that request, I hope," the government man said. Hazard hesitated as Kildare went on: "If we should give up, now, Jerry, it might be the last chance we'll have to rescue Mohra from Wu Fang. Don't you see?"

All the joy that Hazard had experienced left him. In its place there arose the sinister thought of Wu Fang; of his strange hold on the girl that he loved; of the dangers before them, even in this cabin. There was no telling which of these passengers might be Wu Fang's agent. Hazard mentioned the thought to Kildare. The other nodded.

"I'm quite positive we're being watched every second," he said.

They were in the rear of the cabin and commanded a good view of what went on before them. The plane was over the Pennsylvania mountains now, flying toward Ohio.

Hazard's head was spinning from the activity of the last few hectic hours. Kildare noticed his drooping eyes and suggested, "You may as well get some sleep, Jerry. I don't think anything will happen for a while. Suppose you drop off and get some shut-eye? Cappy and I will keep on the watch. Won't we, Cappy?"

"You bet," the boy said.

Hazard laid his head on the rest and closed his eyes, his mind too full of restless thoughts to drop off. He thought of Mohra, of that letter. He found himself still trying to figure out which one of the passengers might be an agent of Wu Fang. There wasn't one that looked other than innocent. He thought of his last visit to Chinatown, of the rats, and the old Chinaman who had killed himself.

After several minutes he opened his eyes, blinked, and glanced at Kildare.

"I can't seem to make it," he said. "I guess my mind is too full of other things to sleep. Why don't you and Cappy try to get some rest, and I'll stay awake. Perhaps later on I can catch a wink or two."

Kildare slumped in his seat. "OK," he said, "but remember, one of us has to stay awake all the time and keep an eye on these passengers."

"I'll stay awake, all right," Hazard assured him. He saw Cappy doze off in front of him and a few minutes later, Kildare slept peacefully.

Hazard studied the passengers. There was something familiar about the face of the beautiful young woman, as she turned to speak to her companion across the aisle. They both had the stamp of Hollywood, and the movies. There was the portly businessman in the last seat ahead of Cappy, probably a German importer. He saw the white hair of the stately old woman protruding above the back of her seat. She must have been a stunning girl in her youth.

Hazard sat up straighter as his eyes turned on another passenger, apparently another businessman. He was dark, with slicked-down hair. He didn't seem at ease. Twice he arose and paced the narrow aisle between the seats. He appeared nervous. Perhaps this was his first trip in an airliner. Then again, perhaps—

Hazard's eyelids closed as the thought came to him. He argued with himself that he was shutting them so that he could ponder that question more thoroughly. Could this man be an agent of Wu Fang? He was the most likely prospect, Hazard decided as he tried to force his eyes open.

Something was happening. The dark man was coming back again, passing down the aisle. He stopped before Cappy and took something from his pocket. A feeling of panic rushed over Hazard as he saw that it was a tiny, deadly thing. He reached out to stop him but he couldn't seem to get there in time.

The man held the snake up and Hazard saw the head leap out toward Cappy, saw the fangs sink into the boy's neck just below the jawbone, where they would strike the jugular vein. Cappy slumped and the dark man turned quickly to Kildare, across the aisle from Hazard. Even yet, Hazard was too paralyzed with horror to move.

He tried to call out. Then the dark, lean man turned upon him, shaking him strangely, his long fingers probing into the pocket where Mohra's letter was stored.

Then Mohra appeared before him. How had she gotten on the ship? Her sad eyes were looking down at him and she was shaking him gently.

"Why did you let him have it, dear Jerry?" she was saying. "Don't you know that Wu Fang will kill me when he finds out? The man was one of his agents. Wu Fang has forgiven me a lot, but he will not overlook this."

Then her voice suddenly changed to a deep, male tone. "Wake up, Jerry! Wake up!"

Jerry Hazard opened his eyes and came out of the fantastic dream with a start. Kildare bent over him, shaking him. But there was no reproach in the government man's face as he said, "Jerry, wake up. I've got something to tell you."

Hazard awoke. "Good Lord, Kildare, I'm awfully sorry. I guess I was sleepier than I thought. Is anything wrong?"

"Nothing more than I expected," Kildare said, "and perhaps it's for the best. We know a little of what we're up against, now."

"What?" Hazard breathed.

"You know the message that Captain Falstaff decoded? I had it in my inside pocket when I went to sleep, but it's gone now."

Jerry Hazard jumped. His brain flashed back to the dream, to Mohra's letter and the dark man who had taken it. He plunged his hand into his inside coat pocket.

CHAPTER 10
MURDER TRANSPORT

TO JERRY HAZARD'S horror, his hand found nothing but an empty pocket. "Why," he said as he stared at Kildare in astonishment, "it's gone."

"What's gone?" Kildare demanded.

"That letter from Mohra."

Kildare shook his head. "That's bad, bad for Mohra at least."

Hazard leaped to his feet. "We've got to do something about it," he said. "We've got to get it back before whoever stole it reads it."

Kildare nodded solemnly. "Yes," he said, "we've got to try, but I'm afraid, Jerry, something more important is going to come up before that."

"What do you mean?" Hazard demanded. "What could be more important than protecting Mohra?"

Kildare answered that in a very low voice. "Getting Wu Fang," he said. "If we get him, we'll protect not only Mohra but every other white person in the world."

"But I don't understand. What do you plan to do?"

"We're going to find out the guilty passenger first," Kildare said. "I think that when we reach our destination, there will be communication between Wu Fang and his agent."

Hazard's eyes lighted instantly.

"I get it," he said. "After we find out who this agent is, we'll follow him."

"That's it. We'll go everywhere he does and eventually we'll find Wu Fang."

"But suppose Wu Fang forces the pilots to fly him to Peru?"

"He can't very well," Kildare said. "They'll have to stop for gasoline, somewhere, or crash in the mountains."

Again Jerry Hazard's thoughts went back to his dream.

"Listen, Kildare," he said, "I think I've got your man." He pointed ahead. "See that dark, slim man? He's just getting up now. I noticed he's been quite nervous since he got into the plane. Here he comes."

Kildare turned and stared, then his face lighted up with a look of recognition.

"Gee, Jerry," he said, "I'm glad you mentioned him. We need to talk to someone we can trust and who was awake while we were all sleeping."

Hazard stared incredulously at Kildare. He was going to ask him what he meant but he held his tongue. Kildare stood up and met the dark man, smiling. They backed away into the little alcove at the rear of the cabin.

"Hello, Bragoni."

The dark man smiled. "Well, damned if it isn't Kildare! Funny I didn't recognize you."

Kildare turned to Hazard and in a low voice, he said, "Bragoni, meet my friend, Jerry Hazard. Jerry, this is Inspector Bragoni of the New York police. Why are you heading for the coast?"

Bragoni shrugged. "I got a guy to pick up in Cleveland. Bank robber, by the name of Harmon."

"You're just the man we want to talk to," Kildare said. "You're after one man and we're after thirteen."

"That ought to be unlucky to them." The New York officer grinned.

"We hope it will be," Kildare said. "Listen, Bragoni. We want to know something. While we were all asleep, a little while ago, something was stolen from our pockets. Can you tell us who came to the rear of the cabin?"

The dark man thought for a moment, then he gave a short nod.

"Don't look now," he said. "She's looking this way."

"Who?" Kildare demanded.

"The old dame," Bragoni answered. "I saw her get up and come back here about twenty minutes ago, but I didn't watch her."

Hazard turned in time to see the elderly woman avert her head and stare out the window. Kildare nudged him in the ribs.

"Don't look at her," he advised. "She's got a mirror before her face on the pretense of powdering her nose, and she's watching us. Well, Bragoni, that seems to be pretty well settled. Let's break up this conference and settle down as though nothing had happened. I'll see you later."

"Sure," Bragoni agreed. "How do you like this air travel, anyway?"

Hazard shrugged and smiled.

"You get used to it rather quickly," he said.

"I hope so," said Bragoni. "This is my first time in the air."

"I noticed," Hazard ventured, "that you seemed rather nervous about it."

"Personally, I'd rather walk," Bragoni smiled. "Well, I'll be seeing you."

WHEN THE plane stopped at Cleveland for gas and to exchange mail, the passengers got out for a rest. Bragoni left on his mission. Then the plane roared on to Chicago.

After the stop at Chicago, Kildare went into the pilots' cabin. He was gone quite some time and Hazard began to worry. He turned to Cappy, who had awakened while they were in Cleveland.

"Stay here, will you, kid?" he said. "I want to go and see what's keeping Kildare."

He glanced at the white-haired old woman and saw her turn a little and watch him calmly as he went down the aisle. She had a large bag lying in her lap, large enough to hold Mohra's letter and the deciphered note that had been stolen from Kildare. He wanted to snatch that bag away from her, but Kildare had issued strict orders against anything of that kind.

He opened the door of the pilots' compartment and stepped in back of Kildare.

"You're just in time, Jerry," Kildare said. He handed him one of a pair of earphones. "Listen."

Hazard put the phone to his ear and he heard a metallic voice coming across out of the ether.

"Everything OK," it was saying. "We got through the storm beyond Wichita. We're flying over the Grand Canyon right now. Ought to be at Las Vegas before long. Clear weather ahead. Everything fine."

"That's Boggs of 1091," Kildare said. "Apparently, Wu Fang has taken command, and you know as well as I do that he won't hesitate to kill both pilots unless they do what he tells them."

He stopped short. Boggs was talking again.

"We are getting near Las Vegas," he was saying. "I can see the airport. Don't expect to land there…. Hello, Las Vegas. Hello, Las Vegas. Don't look for us down. Think we have gas enough to fly to Los Angeles. The passengers want to go on as quickly as possible. We are game to try it, if they want to take the chance."

Kildare was nodding to Hazard.

"Get that voice? You heard Boggs talking back at Newark. Remember he had a very calm voice then? Now it's plenty shaky. I'd bet my neck against a plugged nickel that Wu Fang is standing right behind him, dictating every word."

"But look," Hazard said, "they're apparently not going to try to force them out of the country."

"No," said Kildare, "that's very apparent. It looks as though Wu Fang has given up that idea. He's got some other destination in mind, now. Evidently, he's going to land somewhere beyond Las Vegas and, unless I'm crazy, they'll travel on land the rest of the way. Keep check on their messages," he ordered the co-pilot, "and also their location. Let me know of any change."

"Yes, sir."

Back in their seats again, Hazard leaned across the aisle and spoke to Kildare.

"Can we be sure they're going over Las Vegas?" he asked.

"That's an idea," Kildare said quickly. "I think I'll check on it."

He went forward into the pilots' cabin again. This time he was gone for almost ten minutes. When he returned, the plane was preparing to land in Wichita.

"It's OK," he said. "We just got confirmation from the company's office at Las Vegas that they just saw 1091 go over. That part of it is OK, but they're quite sure that the plane won't have enough gas to make Los Angeles. There's plenty of spaces to land in between Las Vegas and Los Angeles, though."

At Wichita, they got out to stretch their legs. Kildare jerked his head toward the white-haired old lady, who was leaving with the other passengers for a few moments' rest on terra firma.

"Keep an eye on her, will you, Cappy?" he said.

"Don't worry!" Cappy grinned. "I'll keep track of the old dame. She won't get away from me."

"OK." Kildare smiled and patted the boy's shoulder. "Come on, Jerry."

In the company's office at Wichita, Kildare asked about 1091.

"There was something funny about that," said the operations manager. "Boggs, the pilot, came in to make his report here while we gassed him up, and two of the passengers were with him every minute. It looked very much as though they were guarding him to make sure he didn't say something they didn't want him to. The minute he made his report, they went straight back to the plane. Usually, Boggs sits around and chews the fat for a minute or two, but he didn't take time to do that today. He acted kind of nervous and that's not like Boggs."

"See if you can tune in on 1091 now," Kildare suggested.

As he spoke, Hazard saw the white-haired woman enter the dining room. Young Cappy was close on her heels. He winked at the boy and Cappy winked back. Obviously, he was enjoying his role of detective.

After a hasty bite to eat, Kildare and Hazard returned to the plane. It was empty except for the co-pilot.

"Any news?"

"Yes, they're on now," the co-pilot said. "I just got my weather report on beyond Wichita and switched back to 1091. Listen."

He gave earphones to Kildare, who shared them with Jerry Hazard. They heard Boggs' voice.

"We're not going to make it," he said. "We're low on gas. Intend to land just the other side of Death—"

Suddenly, the voice went dead.

A DULL hum came through the earphones. Hazard and Kildare turned questioningly to the pilot, who merely shrugged.

"It looks as though the people in command of 1091 didn't want Boggs to tell where he was setting her down, but he got close enough to it," Kildare remarked.

"Sure," nodded the co-pilot. "He meant that he was going to land just the other side of Death Valley. There's some pretty good landing places there."

The passengers filed back into the plane as Kildare said, "Get out a report at once. Radio the police at Los Angeles to have planes out scouting for the transport between Death Valley and Los Angeles. Understand?"

The co-pilot began to follow instructions.

"Maybe," Hazard said, "we've got the yellow devil cornered."

Kildare shrugged. "I don't know. I'd never bet on it."

The chief pilot crowded past them and took his seat.

"Any objections to running wide open from here to Las Vegas?" Kildare asked him.

"Not if you say so," the pilot answered.

"OK, then, that's the word."

They made record time to Las Vegas and received the same report. 1091 hadn't been heard from since that last word 'Death' which to them had also meant Death Valley. They gassed up quickly as possible and were on their way. They droned high over arid stretches and great wastes of sand.

Suddenly, Kildare cried out, "There it is. See it over there?"

Hazard leaped up and leaned to his side of the ship. He could see a winged thing like a great bird sitting at the edge of a small town.

Kildare rose and started ahead to warn the pilots but they had already spotted it. The plane was nosed down with the motors cut off, and preparing to land.

Hazard had his hand on his gun as they leaped from the ship. They ran toward the great transport where it sat motionless at the edge of a large field. There were townspeople gathered in a huddle.

When they broke through the crowd, they saw two forms lying straight and stiff on the ground, one a lanky individual;

the other shorter and younger. They were clad only in their underclothing.

Someone came up behind Hazard and as he turned, he saw the chief pilot of the airliner and his co-pilot. They were staring at the still forms on the ground.

"Why, it's Boggs and his co-pilot, Merchant," they breathed.

Kildare made a swift examination of the two bodies. Both were dead. He pointed to two tiny fang marks at the backs of their necks where little splotches of blood had clotted. Then he spun around and faced the natives, singling out a brawny ranger wearing a large Stetson hat.

"What happened?" he demanded.

The big fellow answered, "I don't rightly know. We saw this plane come down from the west. When the passengers got out we asked them if there was anything we could do. Then two of them in uniforms—they was the pilots, I guess—said that they had to get some cars and move the passengers on right soon. My boy took the old family bus and started off with a bunch of them and we got some other cars to take the rest. After they left, we started snooping around the plane and found these two fellows lying inside. There was some clothes on the seats, but I don't know whether they were theirs or not."

"They weren't," Kildare snapped briefly. "They exchanged them for the pilots' uniforms. Have you any idea where they've gone?"

"They took the road for Los Angeles," the big fellow told them. "I reckon they're mighty near there by now."

"Have you any other cars left in town?"

"Oh, we all got cars here," the ranger said. "We can sell you gasoline for the plane."

Suddenly Hazard saw Kildare straining his eyes across the field where the planes stood. The government man clutched him and snapped, "Come on. I've spotted something. No, don't hurry. We don't want to let—"

"THE OLD dame!" Cappy cut in excitedly. "Look, she's over there on the other side of the field at the edge of town. She's going down the main street, and she's traveling darn fast, too."

Kildare turned to the pilots. "I'll leave you men to take care of this," he told them. "We're going on after one of your passengers."

With Hazard and Cappy he walked across the field. The white-haired old woman had vanished from sight around a building on the main street. Once, as they turned into the main street, Hazard said, "Good Lord, Kildare, can't we do something about that letter and the note? She's got them both, you know. If we could take care of her and get those two things back, it would save Mohra from getting into trouble and you'd get back Wu Fang's code."

"Yes," said Kildare, "but if we don't let her know that we're following, she'll lead us to Wu Fang. You ought to know by now, Jerry, that if we get him, we'll clean up the whole situation, including Mohra."

They saw the white-haired old lady stop before a garage and talk to a man there. They crouched behind an open car nearby, out of sight.

"Look," Hazard said, "she's trying to hire a car."

A ranger was coming out of a store on the opposite side of the street, crossing to the car behind which they were hidden. As he slid in behind the wheel, Kildare spoke to him.

"There will be a car pulling out of that garage up ahead any minute," the government man said, "and there will be a woman in it who's connected with a couple of murders out here on the field."

The man turned his leathery face toward them in astonishment.

"You mean those two bodies they found in the plane?" he demanded.

Kildare nodded. "We want to follow that car when it starts," he said. "Will you take us? I'll pay you—"

"Well, I ain't rightly in the taxi business," the man said, doubtfully.

"Oh, that part of it will be all right," Kildare assured him. He flashed his badge.

The ranger stared at him. "Say, if you're one of those G-men I've been hearing about, I'll take you for nothing and be glad of the chance."

"All right." Kildare nodded.

As they climbed in, a rather ancient sedan turned out of the garage. The ranger stared at it for a moment.

"You mean to say that white-haired old lady is in on this murder?"

"Exactly," Kildare said.

"Well, say," the ranger said suddenly, "that's Cal Graham

driving that car. I can pull up beside him and tell him what this is all about, if you want me to."

Kildare said quickly, "Don't do that. We want to follow the car and see where she goes. We're after someone else, not her."

"Oh, sure," nodded the ranger. "I get it. You fellows are pretty slick, aren't you?"

"Give them a good lead," Kildare instructed, "so she won't know she's being followed."

The touring car in which they were riding kept well behind the sedan. The driver turned and asked, "Where do you think she's heading for?"

"I don't know," Kildare said, shrugging. "Probably Los Angeles."

Fifteen minutes later the driver exploded, "Hell, Mister, you're wrong. They ain't going to Los Angeles. They just took the right turn that leads into San Francisco."

CHAPTER 11
YELLOW TRAP

TWICE THEY nearly lost track of the old sedan, but each time they caught sight of it and trailed on. As darkness fell, they kept on its tail as they wound through the outskirts of San Francisco in the black of night.

Over the steep hills of the coastal city they traveled, but the ranger showed no signs of weariness. He was a good driver, Hazard observed. The streets were growing narrower as they turned toward the bay.

Climbing along a dimly lighted street, the ranger said, "I don't know all of San Francisco, but it looks to me like they're heading for Chinatown."

"That's what I expected," Kildare said. "As a matter of fact, if you look carefully, you may remember that Chinatown is on top of the very hill we're climbing now. Keep behind that sedan. Whatever you do, don't let it get away."

"Don't worry," the driver said. "I won't."

Hazard stared out at the narrow thoroughfares teeming with Orientals. A little further on, he exploded, "Say, this sure is Chinatown. I thought Chinatown, New York, was quite a place, but Chinatown in San Francisco has it stopped a hundred ways. Why, this is a city by itself."

"Yes," Kildare nodded, "they have their own governing bodies here and everything of that sort. They tell the city of San Francisco what they want in the way of street lamps, paving, and everything else and, believe me, they get it, or there's a riot."

Suddenly he stopped short and stared ahead. The car they had trailed for more than two hundred miles was turning into a steep, narrow thoroughfare. The driver had to throw the car in low gear as he followed the sedan up the incline.

Hazard and Kildare leaned over tensely, staring through the windshield at the car ahead. Suddenly, they saw it stop.

"Switch off your lights," Kildare hissed to the driver, "and we'll wait."

The lights went off, and they stopped some twenty feet behind the sedan. They watched as the white-haired old woman stepped from the car and paid the driver. Then she walked across the narrow sidewalk and stopped before the doorway of a shop, where a dim light glowed.

"Say," said Cappy suddenly, "she's the spryest old dame I ever saw."

Hazard nodded. That thought had occurred to him as he watched her crossing the field back where the two planes had landed. Now she moved with the same quick, panther-like grace.

Kildare turned quickly to the driver.

"I didn't notice the name of the street," he said, "but the number of the store is 163. If you forget that, remember the name, the Curio Shop of San Loy. See it there in the gold letters on the window? The front is barricaded from view by tapestries hung at the window. The light we see comes from above them. You get out of Chinatown, go to a telephone and call the San Francisco police headquarters. Tell them to send a riot squad here at once. I think we're going to need help before we get through."

The ranger swelled with pride at the importance of his mission.

"Yes, sir," he said. "I reckon I'll do that right off as soon as you get out."

"Good," Kildare replied. The old touring car drove off.

Kildare turned to Hazard and whispered, "Have your gun ready."

"Don't worry, it's ready all right."

Two steps took them to the door of the Curio Shop of San Loy. Kildare stopped and peered in the doorway. The old lady

Cappy shot forward with lightning speed.

must have gone inside because they could see no sign of her anywhere.

Kildare tried the door, but it was locked. He rapped on it

gently, three soft knocks. Slowly, the curtain inside the door drew back and a round, yellow face peered out.

"Open up, please," Kildare coaxed. "We would like to look over your tapestries, if you don't mind."

The door opened. A plump, beaming Chinaman bowed as they entered.

"It is very late," he said, "but if you wish, I will show you what I have with pleasure, honorable sirs."

KILDARE STEPPED into the middle of the shop. It was small and dimly lighted from a josh pot on a heavily carved stand beside him. A thick, languid pillar of smoke curled upward, filling the room with a faint Oriental odor. There were other carved tables, fine specimens of Chinese pottery, heavy silk tapestries, embroidered by skillful hands.

"We're looking," Kildare said, "for a certain type of embroidery to exhibit at the art display next week."

The Chinaman bowed again. "I am San Loy," he said. "I will be glad to show you my best specimens. You will sit down, please, and I will have them brought before you."

Kildare dismissed the offer.

"Oh, that's all right," he said. "I'll just go around the room and have a look at all the tapestries."

San Loy bowed courteously. "But it is my custom to serve tea and have the pieces brought before my customers."

"Forget it," Kildare said. Even now he was moving toward the draperies that hung across the back of the shop. Hazard saw him shoot a glance which said as plainly as words, "You stay back toward the front of the shop and have your gun ready."

The newspaperman gave a short nod to show that he understood. He saw San Loy move after Kildare. Instantly, Hazard stepped behind San Loy, but the Chinaman seemed to sense the fact that he was held in a trap, at least for the moment.

Kildare moved from one tapestry to another, inspecting them, feeling them, and ultimately drawing each away from the wall to see if there were any hidden doors behind. He came before a silk hanging, beautifully embroidered, with a great golden dragon upon it. After brief inspection, he pulled it aside.

"Here it is," he exclaimed as he saw a door.

San Loy stepped forward suddenly.

"What are you doing?" he cried.

"You might as well know," Kildare snapped. "A few minutes ago, you let a woman in here. I have an idea she's a beautiful young woman fixed up to look like an old lady."

The Chinaman shook his head.

"No, no," he said. "You are wrong. You are the first to come in here in two hours' time."

"You're a liar," Kildare snarled. "We're going to find her and the man she came to see, if we have to tear up half of Chinatown."

The smile on the round face of the Chinese was gone, and in its place was an ugly snarl. The slant eyes gleamed savagely as he leaped to the side of the room where a long, curved knife hung on the wall.

Hazard saw that movement and tried to jerk the gun from his pocket; but before he could reach it, the Chinaman had the knife out of its sheath and was rushing Kildare. But Cappy was there and he moved with lightning speed. He shot past Hazard in a flying tackle that caught and imprisoned the Chinaman's legs. San Loy raised his great knife to slash down at the head and shoulders of the boy when Hazard rushed in close, catching the man's wrist over his shoulder. Kildare hissed, "Don't shoot. We can't afford to wake up Chinatown at this hour."

Hazard released the wrist of the yellow shopkeeper. His doubled fist came around and connected with the man's paunchy jaw with a smack that echoed soddenly in the drape-covered shop. The blow seemed to have no effect upon the Chinaman. He struggled madly to get his feet and legs free of Cappy's clutching arms. Again Hazard struck, but the blow had no more effect than the first. San Loy could take it.

Kildare came leaping across the carpeted floor with his gun out. It rose and fell with a terrific sound on the skull of the yellow man. The stout body slumped, landing on a thick, Oriental rug that deadened the sound.

Kildare probed into the pockets of the Oriental. Suddenly, he brought out a large bunch of jangling keys.

"Here, give me a hand, Jerry," he said. "We'll drag him over to the corner. That's it."

They half-carried, half-dragged the form of the Chinaman from the middle of the floor to a corner where Chinese rugs were piled in artistic abandon. They laid him on the floor and Kildare threw two of the rugs over him.

"Now," he said, "we'll go into this little matter of trying to find a white-haired woman."

The keys jangled as he moved to the dragon drape and thrust it aside. He found the door locked but he selected a key from the ring, inserted it in the lock, and the door opened easily. He took a small pocket flash from his coat and they entered the dark room.

Evidently, it was the living room of San Loy. A smell of Chinese cooking filled the place, mingled with a faint odor of incense. They moved on toward the other side of the room, where they found another door. That also was locked but opened easily with a key Kildare selected from the ring.

THEY SAW steps leading down, narrow steps that creaked as they walked on them. At the bottom they found themselves in a narrow, winding corridor. Twenty feet farther on, they came to another stairs leading down. Here Kildare stopped, his light beam wavering to the left. A narrow passage branched off from the edge of the stairs. It was little more than a foot wide, scarcely noticeable at first.

Hazard pushed Cappy ahead of him so that he could watch the boy as they moved through this passage. In some places they had to stoop to avoid hitting their heads; at other points, they had to move sidewise to squeeze through it.

"Why are you going this way?" Hazard asked.

"I don't know," the government man answered. "It's just a hunch I got. I figured a place as nearly hidden as this one is must lead to someplace important."

They pushed along, squeezing through the passage that grew still narrower as it went on.

Suddenly Hazard heard Kildare breathe, "God, look at this."

At that, he hurried on after Cappy. The space had suddenly

widened and they were in a little closet-like room, so small that the three of them were cramped for space.

"Sssh," Kildare warned. "Don't say a word. Just look."

Hazard saw him peering through a slit in the wall. The newspaperman moved up beside Kildare and pulled aside the drape that partially covered the opening.

At first, the sight was almost disappointing. He had expected something more illuminating than this. They were looking into an ample, luxuriously-furnished room. Along the opposite wall were bunks. Men of various descriptions were lying on these couches. A young man, whose placid face bespoke good breeding, lay nearest them. Next to him was a hardened old reprobate. A well-dressed Chinaman lay in the next, and the one after that was occupied by an American, evidently down at the heels.

Before each bunk was a stand with certain utensils, including long opium pipes. They were peering into the opium den of San Loy, where poor unfortunates possessed of the ghastly habit came to dream of paradise—only to find hell at the end of the trail.

Farther down, they saw another Chinaman enter and walk to the only vacant bunk in the place. Suddenly, a low gong sounded. A figure glided into the room from behind a drape near where the three of them watched. The figure was that of a young woman, tall, blonde. She moved with an easy grace which Hazard instantly recognized.

Kildare exclaimed, "Look at her! That yellow devil certainly knows how to pick them."

Those words struck a repulsive note on Hazard's ears. He thought of the number of men who must say that about Mohra when they saw her.

"Recognize that walk?" Kildare whispered.

"Yes," Hazard hissed.

"Holy gee," Cappy whispered, "I'll bet she was the old dame we've been looking for."

"I'm sure of it," Kildare shot back.

The beautiful blonde was bearing a tray holding a pipe and other accouterments. She set it on the stand beside the empty bunk to which the Chinaman had retired. It was repulsive to see him stretch out on that bunk, lighting the long pipe with fingers that trembled. Then he lay back, puffing luxuriously at it.

That lovely blonde girl watched him for a moment and then turned to go. Suddenly, she turned her beautiful face to the very tapestry through which the three were staring down at her.

Kildare acted instantly. He pulled the tapestry aside with a quick jerk and stuck the automatic at her.

The government man's voice was low and commanding. "If you move, I'll kill you."

The look of a frightened faun came into her eyes. She stopped, statue-like, staring at them.

As Kildare spoke again, a gong sounded twice, a low and ominous sound that reverberated throughout the room.

"We've got you at last," he rasped. "You and the rest are agents of Wu Fang. I'm going to count ten, and if you don't tell me where he is by that time, I'll shoot you where you stand."

The newspaperman cried out in alarm, "Good Lord, Kildare, you can't—"

A sharp nudge in the ribs silenced him. Kildare was counting rapidly, "One, two, three, four, five, six, seven—"

Suddenly, pandemonium broke loose from behind them. Hazard felt a draft on the back of his neck and he heard something creak as if rusty hinges were being moved. He turned in time to see shadowy forms rushing them from behind and a huge knife flash.

Cappy shouted a warning.

CHAPTER 12
THE SCARLET PLAGUE

TOO LATE, Hazard realized what had happened. Back of where they stood, looking down through the opening, the wall opened as one wide door. It had been built especially so that the agents of Wu Fang could take command of any situation from the balcony. And now, Kildare, Hazard, and Cappy were cornered.

Two knives gleamed in the air above their heads. Kildare and Hazard both carried loaded automatics, but it took time to raise them and fire. The cramped quarters hindered them.

Hazard guessed there must be at least a half dozen brown and yellow men, yelling hideously as they poured through the opening in the wall. He heard Kildare shout something, but the government man was behind him and he couldn't tell above the babbling of their attackers just what he was saying. He saw the leader of the attacking murderers stumble and fall as a small shadowy form dived at the man's running feet. Hazard raised his gun a little higher at the man's chest, ducking a little to the side as he pulled the trigger three times. A great knife grazed his shoulder as it slashed down past him. It hadn't done any damage. The brown man clutched his chest and fell forward.

Another came running over his body with a long, sword-like knife. Now the newspaperman was firing again.

"Where are you, Cappy?" he shouted.

A form was wriggling on the floor under the body of the first brown man that had fallen. That must be Cappy. The others were coming on now so swiftly that Hazard couldn't keep track of them all.

He heard Kildare's voice. It came strangely, as though from a distance. It was pitch-dark in the room. He fired wildly on a level that would take the bullets over Cappy's head if the lad were standing up.

Where was Kildare? Where was he calling from? Why didn't that light shine through the opening from the opium den as it had before? He heard Kildare's voice again and he guessed instantly where it was coming from. Kildare was down below, in the den. He must have jumped through the balcony opening.

"Jerry, Jerry!" he was shouting. "Down here, quick!"

Something swished past Hazard's head in the darkness. He stood with his back to the small draped opening, held his gun high, and emptied it at random into the doorway through which piled the assailants.

"Cappy, Cappy, where are you?" he shouted again. Then he

felt something bump against him and clutch his coat in the blackness.

"Here I am, Jerry," he heard Cappy whisper. "Right beside you."

"Quick!" Hazard snapped. "Climb over the opening and drop into the den. Kildare's down there and he needs help."

At the same moment, he heard three shots ring out below. Light filtered in as Cappy pulled the drape aside and dropped over the side.

Hazard was working frantically, taking out the empty clip and fumbling in his pocket for another one. The attackers yelled as they came on. More of them poured into the little room. It seemed to Hazard that all of Chinatown was pouring through that doorway. The drape that covered the opening vanished. That meant that Cappy had hung on and pulled the curtain down with him.

Hazard could see plainly now in the reflected light. Four still forms lay heaped in the doorway. At least a half dozen more men were swarming into the room over the bodies.

Blam! Blam! Blam!

Hazard's gun echoed and re-echoed again as he jerked the trigger. Spurts of flame leaped at the naked bodies. His bullets found their mark. A thrown knife skimmed by Hazard's ear and thudded into the wood behind him. He let go another volley of random shots. Then, without taking time to see the effect of them, he whirled, crawled through the small opening, and dropped into the den below.

He saw that the opium addicts were apparently peacefully

asleep in their bunks. Kildare was standing with his hand on the wrist of the beautiful girl, holding her tightly. In his right hand he still held his automatic, and he was pointing it at the chest of the young woman.

"Tell me where Wu Fang is before I pull the trigger," he commanded.

The large blue eyes of the beautiful Nordic girl were wide with fear.

"No, no," she protested, "I tell the truth. I do not know where Wu Fang is. I do not—"

Two things happened at that moment. The girl stopped abruptly and the weird, dim light that had illuminated the place went out, leaving them in total darkness. Hazard heard a thudding sound close by and a cry of warning from Cappy: "Look out!" Then, "Mr. Kildare! Mr. Kildare!"

At that, Jerry Hazard took up the cry. "Kildare, Kildare, where are you?" he shouted.

GROPING HANDS seized him. He raised his gun, struck viciously with the butt. A sickening, thudding sound came to him and the clutching hands relaxed. A moment later, he felt Cappy tugging at him with all his might, trying to pull him away. Hazard ran after the boy.

There was no sound now except the gentle, quick padding of many feet on the carpeted floor.

Hazard felt the edge of a bunk and knew that Cappy was pushing him into it. Clever idea, that. They would appear like the other drug addicts. Cappy was in the bunk beside Hazard as he slipped in noiselessly. They lay still there, listening.

"If we only had a flashlight," Hazard groaned to himself. But Kildare had the only one and he had apparently vanished. Perhaps he was dead. The thought panicked him.

The padding of those feet continued. Until now, there hadn't been a word spoken by any of the attackers since the light had gone out. They were moving stealthily about the place, searching for Hazard and Cappy.

Suddenly, the light went on again. Cappy sat up, but the newspaperman lay still and looked about the room. In the center of the floor lay Kildare, stretched out, face down in the thick rug. The girl had vanished completely.

Four half-naked brown men were in the room. They hadn't yet noticed Hazard and Cappy. Hazard was thinking fast, thinking of the possibility of getting all four of them. They passed close to him, looking behind drapes, searching everywhere.

He might get two of them, he guessed, possibly three, but not all four. However, he determined to make the effort and raised his gun. At that moment, the brown man nearest spotted them and let out a cry of alarm.

Blam! Blam!

The automatic bellowed. The Malayan clutched his stomach and fell forward. Now Hazard was pulling that trigger as fast as he could move his fingers, trying to cover the others. He got one. The two remaining turned on him, leaping like great wildcats for his outstretched hand.

Bam!

The light went out. An enormously strong hand grasped his

wrist, his arm went limp, and the gun dropped to the floor. He was being jerked bodily out of the bunk, and as he slammed to the floor, something swished by his head.

He was struggling to get to his feet, but that powerful foe was dragging him across the floor. The more he struggled the more futile his efforts seemed to be. His right arm and shoulder had gone completely numb. His gun was gone, there was no light, and Val Kildare lay stretched out on the floor either unconscious or dead. Apparently, the end was very near for him and Cappy. Wu Fang had won again.

Then all was suddenly changed. Wild shouting filled the place. Beams of light slashed into the room. A police whistle sounded. Shots rang out. The human beast that had been dragging Hazard across the floor let go, uttering a scream of terror as he sprawled across Kildare's body. In the light of the electric torches, Jerry Hazard saw the San Francisco police swarm into the opium den.

"Look behind the drapes!" Hazard shouted to them. "There are doors out of this place. Find a young woman, a beautiful blonde. She must be here somewhere."

Then a great feeling of joy welled over him as he saw Kildare move on the floor. Thank heaven, he wasn't dead! He must have been knocked unconscious.

Other policemen went on with the raid, pulling down heavy drapes, slashing down partitions with axes. But Hazard paid little attention to them now. He heard Cappy's voice ask, "Gee, Mr. Kildare, are you all right?"

Kildare sat up and looked around dizzily.

"Oh, hello, Cappy," he said. "What's up? What happened?" He turned his head to Hazard.

"Are you all right, Jerry?" he asked.

Hazard nodded. Then Kildare looked about the room, still lighted by the torches of the police raiders.

"Where did she go?" he demanded. "Did she get away?"

"Yes," Hazard nodded, "they're looking for her now."

"They'll never find her," Kildare said, shaking his head.

Kildare was right. The police officers tore down partitions, searched passages, ransacked the whole catacomb of underground rooms and dens, but none of Wu Fang's agents were found alive. There were only the bodies of the men that Kildare and Hazard had killed.

Val Kildare spoke only once on the way to police headquarters as they returned with the riot squad. He asked the lieutenant in charge, "How did all this start anyway?"

"We got the word from the down-state ranger that there was some trouble expected here. To hear him tell it, it sounded as though a war was about to break out here in Chinatown."

Kildare nodded. "War would have broken out here," he said, "if there had been enough of us. We tracked Wu Fang all the way to the place of San Loy, but he's gone and I haven't the slightest idea where we'll find him now."

THEY WERE greeted heartily by the police chief of San Francisco. He shook his head when he heard the name of Wu Fang. "Not so healthy, is it?" he ventured. "I've got a lot of confidence in my boys. If it was anyone else but Wu Fang, I'd be inclined to say 'Don't worry, we'll get him,' but there's no one who can compare with that slippery Chinaman. Have you any idea how we can help you, Kildare?"

"No," he said, "I'm afraid I'm stumped. Wu Fang has disappeared completely. If he stays in San Francisco Chinatown, he won't cause us so much worry—at least not on this case."

"What case is that?" the chief asked. "Or don't you care to talk about it?"

"I may as well tell you," Kildare said. He explained the legend of the golden yellow mask that had been handed down through the ages.

"You see," he finished, "there are two dangers from this. If Wu Fang gets hold of the mask and it actually does give the owner strange powers over his subjects, he'll find a way to transfer that power to every yellow man in the world."

The chief smiled. "I'm afraid," he said, "it's too much like a fairy tale for me to have much faith in."

"That," said Kildare, "is because you don't know Wu Fang as well as I do. If this mask hasn't the power that he expects it will have, he'll work out some other method of using it as a bluff. If we can keep him here in Chinatown and prevent him from going to Peru, he'll have a hard time making anything of it."

"Yes," the chief nodded, "I can understand that."

The telephone jangled. The chief picked up the receiver and in a monotonous, disinterested voice, said, "Chief speaking." At length, he said, "Very well, I'll look into it."

Hanging up, he told them, "There's something queer. I'm sure there's no connection between this and Wu Fang, but since we're speaking of Chinamen, you might as well know about it.

The quarantine camp out on the island just informed me that a few hours ago one of the strangest diseases they have ever encountered sprung up in the camp and it's spreading like wildfire among the Chinese."

Kildare leaned forward with interest.

"I didn't get much of it," the chief continued. "It's something about paralysis. The first two Chinese that were afflicted are already dead and the others are dying off fast. I suppose I ought to look into it with the police surgeon. Want to go along?"

"By all means," Kildare said. "To me, it's almost like news from heaven."

"What do you mean?" demanded the chief as they hurried out of the office with Hazard and Cappy close behind.

"In the first place," Kildare said, "I wouldn't count too much on catching this disease. Just be careful not to take anything whatsoever in your mouth while you're there. Don't even take a drink in the quarantine camp."

The chief laughed. "You sound as though you know all about it."

"I know Wu Fang," Kildare countered, "and that's quite enough."

A police boat took them to the island of quarantine. The chief escorted them into the main office and introduced them to the man in charge.

"I think it would be best for the police surgeon to go in first," the chief suggested.

"All right," Kildare said, shrugging.

The doctor left. A few minutes later, he returned with a puzzled look on his face.

"Never saw anything like it in my life," he said.

"Do you think it's contagious?" the chief asked.

"I don't know," said the doctor, shaking his head. "I haven't the slightest idea. At best, the place isn't any too healthy. If you come in, it's at your own risk."

"Have any of the white men been afflicted with this strange disease?" Kildare asked.

"Not so far as I know," the doctor said.

"Then," said Kildare, turning to the chief, "I don't see why it wouldn't be perfectly safe for you to go in. We're going in ourselves."

"Then I'll go with you."

The quarantine doctor escorted them down a short corridor into a room lined with heavy wire. There were bunks and seats in the large open space, and still, in spite of the commodious size, it seemed crammed with Chinamen. They were sitting and talking or walking about the enclosure.

Two of them came to the grating as Hazard and the others entered. One cried, "You must do something for us. You can't leave us here. We'll all die."

"Don't worry," said Kildare, "you aren't going to die. None of you will."

CHAPTER 13
THE RAISING OF THE DEAD

"NOT GOING to die!" the police chief exclaimed. He turned quickly to the quarantine doctor. "Didn't I understand you to say that two of them had already died?"

"Yes." The quarantine doctor nodded with an almost triumphant glance at Kildare. "Perhaps you thought I was kidding you. Since you have been on your way here, two more have died."

Hazard stared at the bunks half-filled with Chinamen who were lying stretched out, motionless. The whole thing was baffling and a little terrifying.

"This room," the quarantine doctor explained, leading the way into another room, "is used generally as a hospital ward, but the plague has come upon us so suddenly that we haven't had time to put it to that purpose. Rather fortunate, too, since it gives us a place to store the bodies as they die. We couldn't take them into the morgue in the city when they have a strange malady like this."

On beds that ranged around two sides of the room, Hazard saw forms lying stretched out. He went over and felt the hand of one of the bodies, drew back quickly in an involuntary gesture of distaste. Then he turned with a frown and jerked his head to Kildare.

"Look here, Kildare," he said. "Feel this hand. It's as cold as the hand of a corpse. You mean to say that these men aren't dead?"

Kildare felt the hand now. Then he slipped his own under the sheet that covered the still form.

"The whole body is pretty cool," he admitted. "How long have they been dead?"

The doctor thought for a moment. "I should say about two hours for that one. He was first to go. Is he cold now?"

Kildare stepped aside as he suggested, "See for yourself."

The doctor nodded and felt the body. "He's dead, all right," he said. "There's no doubt about that."

Kildare drew back the dead man's eyelids. He shrugged and nodded.

"What do you think now?" Hazard asked in a low voice.

"I don't know," Kildare said. "It does look pretty much as though they're dead, doesn't it? And still—" He turned to the doctor. "Have you performed any postmortems on any of these Chinamen yet?"

"No, we haven't had time yet."

"We may as well go," Kildare suggested.

On the way out, he stopped at the desk of the superintendent of quarantine, spoke to the assistant there.

"Tell your boss when he gets in," he instructed, "not to do anything about these Chinamen until he gets in touch with me."

"Yes, sir," the assistant agreed, nodding.

"I think," Kildare said as they went out, "we three had better get a hotel room. I can't see any particular reason for staying awake right now, and we're going to be in for some fun later on. I hope the immigration officials keep in touch with us."

When the police boat brought them back, a taxi drew up before the entrance of the dock. Hazard glanced at the driver. He looked more like a bank clerk than a cab driver.

"I don't like his looks," he commented.

"Nor I," the government man agreed.

They walked past the cab and took the next. Several blocks away, climbing up the steep streets of San Francisco, Kildare looked out of the back window. "We're being followed, all right."

"You mean that cab driver that I remarked about?" he asked.

Kildare nodded. "That's to be expected. I doubt very much if we've made a move in the last four days without being watched." He motioned to a hotel on the right side of the street. "This hotel will do, driver," he said.

IN THEIR suite, a few moments later, Kildare paced the floor. Suddenly, his eyes lighted on the telephone. He put through a call to the quarantine island, got the superintendent on the wire and gave him their temporary address, repeating the admonition to let him know whatever was done in regard to the quarantine prisoners.

He turned to the others. "Let's go down and have a bite of breakfast, and then you two, at least, can turn in. I've got a little figuring I want to do. Then perhaps I'll try to get some sleep myself."

"That," said Hazard, "is right down my street. It's the swellest idea I've heard mentioned in a long time."

After breakfast, Cappy and Hazard turned in for much-needed slumber. Kildare was still puffing at his cigar when Hazard fell asleep.

"Jerry! Jerry!" Kildare's voice came to him from far off. "We've got to hurry. How're your sea legs?"

Hazard sat bolt upright in bed, and Cappy was beside him.

"Gee, are you going to take a sea voyage, Mr. Kildare?" Cappy asked.

"Right," Kildare nodded. "I just called the immigration office at quarantine. Come on, get up and dress. Don't sit there in the bed staring at me. We've got to hurry if we're going to catch that boat."

"Catch what boat?" Hazard asked bewildered. "What are you talking about, Kildare?"

"Just that," Kildare snapped. "Remember I told that assistant at the immigration office to let me know whatever was done with that epidemic over there? Well, I just heard from there now. It seems that when the superintendent of the quarantine island heard about this epidemic, he got all excited and decided to get those Chinamen on a ship immediately and send them back to China."

"But why didn't they call you sooner?" Hazard demanded.

"That," said Kildare, "is what makes me sure that Wu Fang's hand is guiding the whole thing. The telephone wires leading from the quarantine office were cut so that they couldn't get in contact with anyone off the island except by boat. The immigration officer would probably have forgotten to call me anyway in the excitement of the whole thing. But Wu Fang wanted to make sure of it."

Jerry Hazard was still befuddled over the situation. "But I

don't get this, Kildare. What's Wu Fang got to do with the quarantine business anyway?"

"Listen," Kildare said tensely. "Hurry and get your tie and coat on and come along. I'll tell you on the way."

Outside, they found the same cab waiting that had been at the dock. The sleek-looking driver was urgent; but they passed on to the next taxi.

"Drive like the very devil," Kildare ordered the operator.

"Right."

Kildare stared through the back window. "Trailed again," he said briefly.

"Yes," Hazard said, "but what's this you were going to tell us about Wu Fang and the quarantine?"

Kildare turned to him. "Didn't you get the idea on the quarantine island that I suspected Wu Fang of having caused this deadly epidemic?"

"Yes, I got that much of it. But it doesn't make sense, Kildare. He wouldn't do that to a bunch of his own countrymen."

"Don't be silly," Kildare snapped. "Wu Fang has no intentions of killing any Chinaman unless it's absolutely necessary. Those men who apparently died in quarantine haven't died at all. They are now—there's thirteen of them—all in caskets, and have been sent out in the bay to be taken aboard the ship after it weighed anchor. Rather clever, don't you think?"

"I'll be darned if I can see anything clever about it," retorted Hazard.

"Apparently," said a smiling Kildare, "I shouldn't have let you sleep so long. Here's what's happened. Every possible means of

Wu Fang's getting out of the country has been cut off. He couldn't bribe or scare Boggs and his co-pilot to fly him out of the country, so when they landed to gas up, he killed them. He came to Chinatown with a purpose and found that there were two or three dozen Chinamen held in quarantine who were trying to enter the country as visitors. In some way—don't ask me how—he managed to inflict them with what seems to be a strange malady. To all appearances, they died. But in reality, they're just as alive as we are."

"I don't see yet," Hazard said with a shake of his head, "what that has to do with our sudden sea voyage."

"Simply this—Wu Fang has been looking for a way to get out of the country without telltale passports. He knows every means of escape is being watched. Through agents of his on the immigration island, possibly the interpreter, he smuggled in a drug that paralyzes at first and then stills all the organic functions in the human body, so that it appears dead."

"But that's impossible, isn't it?" Hazard demanded.

"Not to Wu Fang," Kildare assured him. "I just got word from the immigration office that those thirteen dead Chinese are on a freighter bound for China."

"**BUT YOU** left orders—" Hazard began.

"Yes, yes," the government man said. "I know. But remember, the telephone connections were cut and they just got them repaired. Unless I'm crazy, we'll find Wu Fang and his twelve agents in those thirteen caskets. He tried that once before and got away with it, but he won't this time if we can get to the ship."

Hazard's mind flashed back to the Newark airport. There had been thirteen passengers aboard the ship. And the only woman on board had answered to the description of Mohra.

"Good Lord!" he cried. "Do you think Mohra is in one of those caskets, Kildare?"

Kildare nodded, tight-lipped.

"Yes," he said, "I'm afraid so, Jerry."

A wild anguish welled inside Jerry Hazard. He yelled to the driver.

"Drive as fast as you can! Don't stop for anything. There's a life at stake!"

"In fact, there are thousands of lives at stake," Kildare chimed in.

The taxi driver turned his head and spoke out of the corner of his mouth.

"What do you think I am, an aviator?" he demanded. "I've got her down to the floor now, and there's a speed cop on my tail."

"Keep going," Hazard snapped, "We'll take care of the cops." He looked back now and saw that the cop was drawing alongside. That other taxi was there, too, a half block behind.

Kildare stuck his head from the cab window as the motorcycle cop yelled, "Hey, you! What're you trying to do, break a record?"

He flashed his badge. "It's a case of life and death, officer. Stop that cab behind us and ask the driver for his license. I think you'll find he's driving without one."

The motorcycle turned and started back.

132

The cop motioned the other cab to the curb.

"What do you figure to do?" Hazard demanded as they raced on. "You say the boat's gone already?"

"She left a little less than an hour ago," Kildare said. "She must be almost through the Golden Gate by now. We'll have to get a fast cruiser to take us out to her."

They found a fast cruiser at the docks. They chartered it and set out in hot pursuit of the fleeing Chinese.

"What's the name of the ship," the skipper of the cruiser asked.

"It's the American freighter, Ocola," Kildare said.

They scanned the horizon in vain. Suddenly, Hazard spotted a line of smoke out through the Golden Gate.

"Is that it?" he asked.

"More than likely."

The fast cruiser ploughed through the waves past the Golden Gate. They could see the freighter now, out across the sea.

"What do you think Wu Fang will do?" Hazard asked. "He certainly doesn't intend to go to China on that ship."

"Don't worry," Kildare said, "he won't. He'll overpower the crew and take possession of the ship and then head for Peru."

The space between the two craft narrowed all too slowly for Jerry Hazard. He was up in the bow of the cruiser. The position made him feel a little nearer to the one who was dearer than life itself to him.

As they pulled alongside the freighter Ocola, members of the crew leaned over the rail and shouted down, "You can't come aboard here."

Kildare pulled back his coat and showed his badge of authority.

"Drop a rope," he shouted. "We're coming aboard anyway. We're not afraid of this epidemic you've got on board."

The captain came to the rail and stared down with one eye cocked. Then he snapped orders to the crew and a rope ladder was dropped.

JERRY HAZARD was the first man over the side. Cappy came next, with Kildare behind him. Kildare waved the express cruiser away and then turned to face the captain. He told him in a few words what he knew.

The captain—his name was Malloy—listened with apparently mild interest, his eyes narrowing when Kildare told him of his belief that Wu Fang himself was on board.

"So you think that yellow spalpeen is on board here, do you?" he roared. "Well, we'll soon find out, and believe me, when we catch him, we'll finish him off right. I'd just like to get my hands on that yellow devil. Have you any idea where he might be hiding?"

Kildare was inspecting his automatic. "I think the first place to look is inside the thirteen caskets."

"All right, sir," nodded the captain. "We'll look in the caskets." He grinned at Kildare suddenly. "If you don't mind my saying so, sir," he said, "you do think of the nicest places to look."

Kildare asked, "Where are these other Chinamen, the ones that aren't dead?"

"Oh, they're up in some extra quarters in the stern of the ship. And believe me, I've got them locked up, too. They aren't going to get out until we get to China. Come on, let's take a look at those coffins."

They reached the bottom of the stairs and found themselves in a small, stiflingly hot room.

"This is just above the boilers," the captain explained. "It will be cooler below."

He led them to another flight of stairs, and deeper into the hold of the ship. At the bottom, he reached a switch and a light glowed dimly. Great piles of boxes and crates were heaped along the hold with narrow passages between them. The captain led the way down one of these passages to the bow of the ship.

"We stuck all the stiffs up here in the front," he said. "They're lighter than the rest of the cargo."

Kildare stopped short. "Have you got some pinch bars we can use to pry open these caskets?"

The captain nodded and turned to the side, where a great beam went up to support the ceiling above. There were pinch bars, crowbars and wooden poles here. The captain took some down, handed them around.

"Be ready with these clubs," Kildare said. "They kill more effectively than automatics, particularly when the thing you're after is so small that you can't hit it with a pistol."

Armed in this fashion, they advanced upon the thirteen caskets.

"Is this the way you placed them here?" Kildare asked.

"I guess so," the captain answered. "Let's take a look inside."

They pried off the covers of the plain wooden boxes. Hazard's cover came up. He stared inside the wooden box, an amazed expression on his face.

"Damn!" he heard Kildare exclaim. "Just as I expected. They're empty!"

CHAPTER 14
DEATH CARGO

TO HAZARD, the amazing situation in which they found themselves was more than ominous. There could be no doubt that Kildare was right in his contention that Wu Fang and his twelve agents were aboard. Although he had hoped against his better judgment that it wasn't true. Now, these empty caskets were convincing proof. The Dragon Lord of Crime was loose. With it all came the ghastly thought that down there somewhere, perhaps hiding in a veritable rats' nest, was Mohra.

Kildare didn't seem surprised. He began prying the lid off the next casket.

"Come on, Jerry," he said, "you look as though you'd seen a ghost. We've got to make sure there aren't any of Wu Fang's agents left in here. You certainly didn't expect to trap them in these caskets, did you?"

Hazard was still grasped in astonishment. He simply stood, staring into space.

Captain Malloy exclaimed angrily as he ripped off the lid of his first coffin.

"This is the strangest thing that ever happened on any ship that I've been on," he said. "If they weren't sending good empty caskets to China, I wouldn't think anything of it, but these are just plain wooden boxes. Why, suffering cats, the Chinese could make these boxes over there for one tenth of the cost. What's the sense of—"

"There isn't any sense to that end of it," Kildare interrupted him. "There were bodies in these caskets when they came aboard. I'm positive of that. They—"

He stopped short and stared at the casket before him. He had made two jabs at the lid already, but it resisted his efforts. Now he stood there, looking strangely at the long, narrow box.

Suddenly he lifted it from the floor, turned it over, and dropped it on its side. The bottom fell out and the great hold of the ship echoed with its hollow thud.

"There's the answer," he exclaimed triumphantly. "I've been trying to figure out how they got out and replaced the lids so securely without leaving any marks. Look here. They have a trick spring arrangement that secures the bottom in such a way, it can be unfastened from inside."

He moved to the next casket and the same thing happened there. Now they were hurrying on to the others, tipping them up, and letting the bottoms drop out of the vacant death boxes. All thirteen were empty.

As Hazard helped, the thought of Mohra was uppermost in his mind. He could hear her voice over and over again, saying, "Dear Jerry, if you love me." He groaned inwardly as he thought of the girl's lovely body stretched in one of those boxes lifted and lowered into the hold.

"Good Lord, Kildare," he burst out in anguish, can't we do

anything to free Mohra from this awful situation? She's somewhere in the hold of this ship."

"We're going to do as much as we can," Kildare said through clenched teeth. "At least we've got all day to search the ship. We'll tear every packing case apart if we have to, to find Wu Fang and his devils."

"I think," he added, "there's only one thing to do. How many have you got in your crew, captain?"

Captain Malloy answered immediately, "There's nine of us, including me."

Kildare shook his head but said nothing. Instead, he turned and strode through the hold the way they had come. "Hey, where are you going?" the captain demanded. "I thought you were going to start searching the hold right now!"

Kildare continued walking toward the entrance. In a conspicuously loud voice, he said, "No, it wouldn't do any good. I'm afraid we're in for it. If we tried to search this hold, we would all be killed. Come on. Let's get out of here while we're still alive."

HE BROKE into a run through the line of crates and cases piled high all around them. Cappy was the first to follow. The captain held back, but Hazard pushed him in front of him and motioned him forward.

"Let's go," he whispered. "Kildare knows what he's taking about."

Captain Malloy moved ahead, unwillingly, and Hazard followed close upon his heels. He had the feeling that eyes were upon him, staring from dark recesses between the packing cases.

They hadn't followed Kildare's suggestion any too soon. Before they reached the steep iron stairs that led into the hold itself, the dim lights that Captain Malloy had switched on when they had entered went out.

Kildare uttered a second warning. "Look out!"

The boom of his automatic echoed twice in the great space below, and Hazard saw two tiny darts of flame leap forward.

"Confound it!" he heard Kildare exclaim angrily. "I missed him. Quick! Follow me up the stairs."

The captain rushed for the iron steps and dashed up without any further urging. An instant later, the lights went on again. Malloy was standing halfway up the stairs with his hand on the switch; he shook with rage.

"Wait until I get my hands on that spalpeen," he rasped. "I'll show him what happens to yellow devils that go turning off lights on my ship without the captain's orders."

Hazard pushed him up the stairs.

"Get going, captain," he demanded. "We can't do any good down here in the hold—alone."

But Captain Malloy was in an argumentative mood and he stood his ground.

"I'm going back," he said, "and lick those devils with my bare hands."

Hazard thought fast. He had to get the captain up those stairs and out of his way as soon as possible.

"Run up the stairs, then, captain," he said. "The man that turned off the lights went up ahead of Kildare."

"Oh he did, did he?" the captain flared. "Well, I'll have my crew after him in less than ten seconds, and when we catch him—"

The captain's words faded away as he ran for the next staircase that led onto the deck. He yelled, and his crew came on the run. Hard looking sailors, they were, rough, tough and ready. They were grinning happily in anticipation. The captain said, "There's a dead man come to life in the hold, out of one of those coffins. He came up out of the hold just now. I want you to search the ship and when you find him, bring him to me."

Kildare turned and eyed the captain strangely.

"How do you know he came this way?" he demanded. "Did you see him?"

"No," Captain Malloy said, shaking his head, "but your partner said he came up this way."

Kildare smiled and turned to Hazard.

"That was a good guess, Jerry," he said. "I saw him rather dimly on the stairs as I was staring up. He switched off the lights just as I spotted him and I took a couple of shots at him. But when I came up to where his body should have been, it wasn't there."

"What did he look like?" the captain demanded.

"I couldn't see him plainly," Kildare said. "I just saw the form on the stairs. Is there any other way down to the hold besides this, captain?"

"Yes," the captain said. "There are two other ways. We went down out of the middle of the ship, but there's a stairway forward and aft."

The crew had scurried away in search of the marauder.

"Now that we're alone," Kildare said, "I'll tell you why I got out of the hold so quickly. For one thing, I heard a sound behind a row of freight between us and the stairs. That meant things would begin to happen any minute. We were away from the light switch, and if they trapped us in the hold with only four of us, against thirteen of them, we wouldn't have a chance.

"I spoke as loudly as I could down there to give them the idea that we were not going to search the hold. I thought that would throw them off for at least awhile.

"Now I'll tell you what I think would be the best thing to do. There's you and your crew and the three of us. That makes twelve altogether against thirteen of them, not counting all the ghastly little beasts that in all probability Wu Fang has brought with him."

He stopped for a moment and stared out beyond the after part of the ship. Already they were out of sight of land.

"We're out on the Pacific," he said, "and we're in a dangerous spot, but there's still quite a bit of daylight left and we've got a chance. My suggestion is that we radio the police in San Francisco and tell them to bring an ample riot squad on two police boats. Then I would suggest that we turn your ship about and head back."

Captain Malloy's face darkened at that proposal.

"You mean," he demanded, "that you want me to admit to the police that I can't handle anything that comes up on my ship?"

Kildare shook his head and said, "No, that's not it at all, captain. It's simply this. No matter what you think of your ability, this ship will not be run by you and your crew. You will lose control of it within twenty-four hours. I'll give you all due credit, captain, for being able to handle ordinary men on a sea voyage, but you can take my word for it that Wu Fang and his agents are no ordinary humans. They'll get what they want even if they have to kill all twelve of us to do it. As a matter of fact, nothing would please Wu Fang better."

KILDARE SAW the captain hesitate. He went on with another warning.

"When darkness comes, captain, you'll wish you had taken my advice, but we'll be too far out to sea to get help by that time. We've got to see this thing through right. This is the greatest chance we've had to catch Wu Fang and his agents red-handed. There'll be some of us killed even though we do get the police to help, but at least we'll have the satisfaction of having Wu Fang and his agents in mid-ocean and pretty well cornered."

As Kildare finished his plea, a crashing sound came from up forward.

"What's that?" he demanded.

The crashing sound came again, and continued.

"Sounds like something's being broken up," the government man said.

The captain's face lighted up in a smile. "It sounds more like a fight. Come on, follow me."

They raced up two flights of stairs to the bridge. Behind the bridge several doors led to cabins; some were open, some closed.

The crashing ceased as they ran up the last flight. Hazard,

who was bringing up the rear, saw the captain dart into one of the open doors. The next instant they were all inside, staring with amazement.

Hazard's eyes riveted on the wireless panel and the instruments that controlled it. Once there had been dials there and tubes and earphones and keys. Now the table and the panel on the wall were shattered to bits and there were wires hanging and smashed instruments lying about the place. A man lay stretched out on the floor. Kildare bent over him.

"One of Wu Fang's jobs," he said. Then he lifted his head, looked at the captain.

"Well, captain, there's your wireless apparatus. You'll never send another message over that again. Wu Fang has done his job well. We're completely out of touch with the rest of the world."

The captain's mouth was open as he stared with baffled rage at the havoc that had been wrought in so short a time.

Kildare darted to the other side of the cabin.

"This is the way," he snapped. "Come on."

The captain followed, uttering violent oaths and curses; but he became speechless with rage as he stood before the doorway of the pilot house. Another form lay stretched on the floor, and the wheel was swinging back and forth, back and forth, aimlessly.

"They got Olsen, my pilot," the captain groaned. He leaped to the wheel and steadied it as Kildare and Hazard stared down at the compass. It pointed almost due north.

The captain jerked his head back toward the body of the pilot.

"Look him over and see how long he's been dead," he said.

Kildare turned and began feeling the body. A moment later, he looked up. "Not long. Maybe it's two minutes or perhaps twenty, certainly not longer than that."

The captain scowled.

"Do you know where we're headed?" he asked. "We're going straight toward Alaska."

"Alaska!" Kildare exploded.

"That's what I said," the captain replied. "We're heading due north."

He turned the wheel gently and the great freighter began turning to the left. The compass swung slowly to 254 degrees, a little south of due west.

"There," the captain said with satisfaction, "that's better." He turned to Cappy. "Go and find Simmons among the crew."

Cappy nodded and trotted off. A few minutes later, a small, weather-beaten man came up and the captain handed the wheel to him. Then he gave Kildare his final decision.

"This is my ship," he said. "We've got a cargo to take to China and we're going to take it there. You can mark my word, these yellow devils aren't going to stop us and we're not going to ask the police for help, either. I'm master of my own ship and that's that."

He gave Kildare, Hazard, and Cappy a cabin for their use during the voyage.

"Apparently," Kildare observed when they were alone, "there's nothing we can do. Captain Malloy is master of his ship. There's no doubt about that, but I think that after tonight he'll wish he had taken my advice."

KILDARE AND Hazard took turns on watch till dawn arrived. Nothing happened. The Pacific lay calm and majestic.

Kildare looked baffled. "It's beyond me," he said. "To tell the honest truth, Jerry, I hardly expected that any of us would live the night out. I can't figure the thing out. I must have been wrong in my guess."

"You mean that Wu Fang isn't on board?" Hazard asked quickly.

"No," Kildare told him. "I'm just as positive of that as I was yesterday afternoon, but it's the fact that he's so quiet. I figured that he and his agents would take command of the ship by killing off the crew and the rest of us so they would have a free hand to go to Peru. But that doesn't seem to be the case. I just checked the compass course. Simmons is still at the wheel but he'll be relieved shortly. He said everything was going smoothly."

And so it went, for seven long, nerve-wracking days. Peace and quiet—with the ship ploughing through the Pacific under leaden skies. The heavy clouds had not lifted once since the Ocola had left port, but there was no rain.

Now and then, Captain Malloy took occasion to chuckle and say, "You've got nothing to worry about as long as I'm captain of this ship. Didn't I tell you so at the start?"

Kildare shook his head and said, "You win, Malloy—so far."

But Jerry Hazard's nerves were straining. He had perfect

145

confidence in Kildare's deductions, and he was sure himself that Wu Fang was on that ship. But why didn't he do something? And, as always, his thoughts would return to Mohra. He hadn't a doubt that she was on that ship hidden somewhere in the cargo in the hold.

On the eighth night, when Hazard's nerves were so frayed that he couldn't sleep, could do nothing but pace the deck and think and wonder, Wu Fang showed his hand. Hazard stood in the bow of the ship, facing out across the ocean, trying to tell himself as he had tried a thousand times before that Mohra was all right; that she was back in San Francisco; that Wu Fang and his agents were not on board. Suddenly, he heard a step behind him. He turned. He couldn't see the face in the darkness, but he recognized immediately the slim, graceful form that glided toward him. It was a figure clad in overalls with a rough seaman's cap pulled well down over the face. Instantly, he breathed the name, "Mohra!"

CHAPTER 15
CAPTAIN MURDER

"SSH," SHE cautioned. He felt her breath on his cheek as she whispered, hotly, "I can only stay for a minute; you must not speak aloud and you must not try to stop me."

A million things welled up in Hazard's throat. Words stumbled in an effort to escape his lips. But Mohra was racing on, speaking in her gentle whisper.

"You received my message," she said. "I am sure you did

because the boy is with you and it was given to him. But you did not heed my warning. I will not ask you why, Jerry. There isn't time. But I am glad that you came, even though you are about to be placed in the most dangerous position of your life. I think more of you for not staying behind, Jerry."

In one swift, sure movement, Jerry's arms were about the girl and he was drawing her close, brutally close. Although his mind was filled with a thousand questions, his lips would only repeat, "Mohra darling, Mohra darling," over and over again.

Mohra clung to him for a second, her soft hands caressing his face and neck. Their lips were close, almost touching. Suddenly, she pushed him away.

At that, suspicion possessed Jerry Hazard. It suddenly dawned that Mohra had come with a purpose, strange and unexplainable, and now that she had accomplished her mission, she was repelling him. He held her close for another instant. Then, he released her and she stepped away from him.

"You must trust me, Jerry," she breathed. And in spite of his sudden distrust, he realized that the girl's voice was unmistakably trembling.

"Mohra, we've got to make the break now," he pleaded, desperately. "You can't leave me. You've got to stay. I—I can't go on like this, realizing that you—"

Mohra stopped a little farther away from him in the dark shadow of the deck.

"No, no, please don't, Jerry," she pleaded. "You've got to trust me. You've got to stay here and let me go. I have something to do, something that vitally concerns you—and the others. You must be patient. I shall be hoping for your safety tonight, hoping and—"

She stopped abruptly, turned like a wild thing that had suddenly taken fright and ran back along the bulwark of the deck into the deep shadows.

Hazard followed for a few paces. Then he stopped. There had been something in the way she had spoken that made him trust her and kept him from following any further. Now, as he stared ahead, she was gone.

He wasn't quite sure how long he stood there, staring up toward the dark hole beneath the bridge where she had vanished. His brain spun dizzily with a million thoughts and apprehensions.

Things had been much too peaceful during those eight days and nights. But on this eighth night, something was going to happen. There could be no doubt of that; Mohra had practically told him so.

He moved aft along the forward deck. Unconsciously, his feet took him to the cabin where he had left Kildare and Cappy. He found Cappy sitting on the edge of his bunk, rubbing his eyes sleepily, and Val Kildare pacing the floor in his pajamas.

"Have you seen Mohra?" Kildare demanded.

The newspaperman frowned. How did Kildare know he had seen her? Had they been spying on him? He nodded affirmatively.

"She's been here, too," Kildare said.

"Been here?"

"Yes. I was about half asleep when I heard Cappy mumble and then cry out. I was pretty sure he wasn't dreaming."

"Gee," Cappy said, "I was scared. Something woke me up and I felt hands rubbing my neck. I guess I must have thought somebody was choking me. Then I heard a woman's voice say, 'Ssh. I'm Mohra. I am here to help you. Don't cry out.'"

"But you see," Kildare explained, "he had already called my name. I reached under my pillow for my automatic and sat up. I was just going to shoot when I heard Mohra's voice. She whispered, 'Mr. Kildare, is that you? I must see you.' I slid off the bunk and stood in front of her. I must admit that I was pretty surprised, so much so that I left my gun at my side."

"I think that was because you trusted Mohra," Hazard ventured. "Isn't that it?"

Kildare hesitated a moment. Then he nodded.

"Maybe you're right," he said. "At any rate, she did a very strange thing as she stood before me in the darkness. She said, 'I am here to help you and you must trust me.' She whispered that so low that I could scarcely catch the words. Then I saw something flash through the air and the next instant she slapped me on both cheeks with her hands. It wasn't a stinging blow, just hard enough so that I realized she didn't mean it for a caress. Then her hands passed swiftly over my neck. I asked her what she was doing but she only repeated, 'You must trust me.' I reached for the light then, but when I turned it on, she was gone."

"You didn't try to follow her?" Hazard asked.

"No," Kildare said, shaking his head. "I don't know just why, but I guess what you said explains it. I believe I do trust her, absolutely."

Cappy was rubbing his cheek and neck with his hands like a man who had just escaped being strangled. Suddenly, Kildare leaped across the room and pulled his hands down.

"I wouldn't do that," he said hoarsely.

Cappy looked at him in amazement.

"Do what, Mr. Kildare?" he asked.

"Rub your face with your hands."

"What do you mean?" Hazard asked.

"I DON'T exactly know, Jerry," he admitted. "Maybe it's just a hunch I have, but I don't think either of us should touch our faces and necks where Mohra touched us with her hands. Did you see Mohra too, Jerry?"

Hazard hesitated before answering. Perhaps it was embarrassment. He was thinking of what had happened there on the deck, of Mohra caressing him and then leaving him so abruptly with the same plea she had given Kildare, "You must trust me."

But Kildare's gray, level eyes were upon him, questioning him. "Yes, I saw Mohra," he said. "She came up to me on the forward deck."

"She didn't," Kildare suggested, "slap you in the face, did she?"

Hazard shook his head. "No," he said, "that is—"

Kildare leaned forward in sudden eagerness. "But she did touch your face and neck with her hands, didn't she?" he asked.

"Yes," Hazard admitted.

"I see," Kildare said thoughtfully. "It wasn't exactly a slap in the face, but more of a caress, eh, Jerry?" He smiled. "Never mind answering that, Jerry. I know how you feel and I don't

151

blame you. But what did she say that would affect the rest of us?"

"I think something is coming off tonight," Hazard answered.

Kildare nodded. "What else did she say?"

Hazard thought for a moment. "Why—why nothing. That is, nothing that would concern you and Cappy."

Suddenly, they heard feet pounding on the deck outside the cabin. As Hazard turned toward the door, it burst open and Captain Malloy plunged in.

"Kildare!" he shouted. "We've been tricked. Come outside. I want to show you something."

Kildare followed the captain out, Hazard and Cappy trailing. The captain pointed into the sky.

Hazard noted that for the first time during the voyage the sky was clear in spots. They could look between the drifting clouds and see stars winking down at them.

Captain Malloy pointed at one, a star that shone brightly, almost directly above the Ocola's stern.

"See that star, Kildare?" he said. "Do you know what it is? That's the north star. We've had solid clouds over us ever since we left San Francisco and we haven't been able to take our bearings except by compass. Now there's the north star, astern of the ship. Know what that means?"

Hazard was just getting the idea as Kildare spoke.

"If the north star is on our stern," he said, "we're headed—" He stopped, suddenly, then exploded, "God, man, we're headed south!"

"That's right," the captain nodded. "Instead of heading for

China as we should be, we're headed for South America. We've been traveling eight days in that direction, now, with the compass telling us we're headed for China."

Kildare darted into the cabin. When he returned he had his automatic in hand.

"Come on," he said grimly, "lead the way. We're going up to the pilot house and see what's wrong with the compass. I think I know already."

"You do?" demanded the captain.

"Yes. Come on and I'll show you. No wonder we haven't been molested during these eight days."

They followed him toward the pilot house. Kildare was first and Cappy was behind him, with Hazard and the captain bringing up the rear. Kildare was almost at the entrance when they heard him shout, "Look out!"

At the same time, Hazard heard the sound of swishing wings, the same sound he had heard on Long Island, the night that Falstaff had his throat torn to ribbons. He ducked instantly, pushing Cappy ahead of him. From behind Hazard came a deep-throated roar of rage and pain. He saw Captain Malloy's body moving and swaying in the darkness. He was clutching and fighting at something that Hazard couldn't make out. But it was something that seemed to be flapping.

"Down everybody!" Kildare barked.

As they dropped, Kildare's automatic boomed. Two darts of flame shot from the muzzle of the gun.

There was a high-pitched screech. The captain was gurgling and cursing as he fell to the deck. Kildare shot twice more into the air. Hazard had his own gun out but couldn't tell definitely just where that whir of wings was coming from.

Suddenly, a light glowed in Kildare's hand and he was racing back and turning over the captain's body. Hazard saw it was still twitching, blood spurting like a geyser from the throat, the flesh of which was torn away.

Kildare leaped up from his crouched position beside the captain's body.

"Quick!" he yelled. "Into the pilot house. Simmons is there at the wheel."

As he turned, a piercing cry came out of the night from high in the crow's nest. Kildare stopped and stared. "Look!" he shouted.

HAZARD SAW it too, the form of a man tumbling through the night. Appalled at the ghastly sight, he heard the swish of wings some distance away.

Blam!

The deck shuddered as the body of the falling seaman struck it.

"Into the pilot house, everybody!" Kildare repeated. "We can't do anything here."

They charged into the little enclosure and ran smack into Simmons, who had left the wheel to run out.

"What happened?" he asked.

"Never mind, now," Kildare snapped. "We haven't time to talk. Where's the switch? We want lights in here and all the windows closed. Quick!"

When the lights were switched on, Hazard saw an open

window before the wheel. He leaped and closed it with a bang while Kildare attended to the other window in the room.

As Kildare stared at the great compass before the wheel, Simmons demanded, "What in the name of all hell is going on here?"

"Murder," Kildare snapped back. "Death is walking the Ocola's decks tonight. The captain and two of the crew are gone already."

Simmons stared at him as though he were crazy. Suddenly he whirled for the door, but Hazard grabbed his arm.

"If you value your life," he barked, "don't go out there."

"Stay here by the wheel," Kildare snapped. "Do you know where we're headed?"

Simmons was angry now rather than frightened.

"What are you trying to do, kid me?" he snarled.

With that, he jerked out a revolver and swung around, his back to the glass at the side of the pilot house.

"I'm onto you, now," he growled, addressing Kildare. "You come on board flashing a badge, and tell us there's some Chinks on board that are going to take over the ship, and it's you that's after it all the time. I—"

A scream of panic sounded in the night. A pounding of feet on the deck was followed by another scream.

"Five," said Kildare between clenched teeth.

"Yeh," rasped Simmons, "and you're behind it all. Make one false move and I'll plug you. Don't forget I'm close enough not to miss."

Kildare faced Simmons calmly. Hazard was boiling inside.

He wanted to get this ridiculous argument over with, but he knew that the pilot wouldn't hesitate to drill him if he moved.

"Listen," Kildare said. "You think we've been heading for China, but ever since we left San Francisco, there's been a solid cloud bank covering the sun, moon, and stars. It's just broken away tonight. Take a look at the sky behind the ship. If there aren't any clouds in the way now, you'll see the north star. That ought to bear out what I have just said. We're pointing toward South America. As a matter of fact, I wouldn't be a bit surprised if we were only a little off the coast of Peru."

Simmons uttered an oath, still keeping the gun trained on the three inside.

"I think you're lying," he rasped. "If that north star is off our stern, I'll come back and shoot all three of you. That will mean that you've tampered with the compass."

He backed out of the pilot house and merged into the darkness. Hazard leaped after him to draw him back a second time. There came the swish of wings. He fired hastily at something that charged down on Simmons, a small winged thing. The sounds of ripping flesh, gushing blood, and Simmons' agonized screams all mingled, to make a hideous uproar.

Hazard shot three times at the winged thing that was diving to the kill. Each time he missed. Out of the tail of his eye, he spotted a figure climbing the rail. Instantly, he swung his gun around to shoot, but the automatic didn't go off. In fact, he didn't even pull the trigger.

Suddenly, he felt the sting of something like a needle in his right arm and heard his gun clatter to the deck. Paralysis swept over him. The fingers of his left hand were numb.

He heard Cappy cry out, "Jerry! Jerry! Are you all right?" HAZARD'S BRAIN, eyes, and ears seemed to be perfectly normal. He tried to cry out a warning to the others, to tell them to stay back in the pilot house, but he couldn't make his lips move.

Cappy came out of the pilot house but could only stand there like a marble statue. He saw the queer figure that had come over the rail, stand shrouded in the darkness, waiting for the next victim. There seemed to be a blow pipe between the teeth of the grotesque human being.

Kildare raced out of the pilot house. "I found it!" he shouted. "They had a magnet hidden near the compass that must have changed it to point about ninety degrees away from north."

Hazard saw Kildare's light flash on and knew that the beam was striking him in the face.

Kildare cried out, "What's happened to you, Jerry? You look as though—"

Suddenly, he stopped short. As he spoke, Hazard heard the swish of something whizzing through the air, and saw Kildare fall. Cappy was running toward him when suddenly he, too, stopped and went rigid.

That seemed to be a signal. Dark forms rushed over the deck from every direction, charging at them. Strong, powerful hands grasped Hazard, picked him up, and carried him away. He heard the soft padding of other feet behind him, and he knew that Kildare and Cappy were also being carried through the darkness.

From down the deck there came a gurgling cry, ending in a choked-off gasp. Next, Hazard heard the splash of a body being thrown into the water.

He could see the faces of the men who carried them back into their own cabin. One had a yellow face, horribly scarred on one side. The other was a white man. Two swarthy men entered, bearing Cappy between them. The boy's eyes bulged a little, but there was little fear in them. Next, three dark-skinned, half-naked Malayans bore Kildare in.

Kildare's eyes traveled swiftly about the cabin interior, but he, like Hazard and Cappy, had no power of speech. They dropped Kildare unceremoniously to the floor and left them alone for a moment.

A tall, yellow, slope-shouldered figure appeared in the light of the room. His forehead was high and wide, his face long, his lips thin and cruel as they parted in a smile. He wore a long yellow silk robe and carried a small, heavily carved box. Wu Fang, the Dragon Lord of Crime, stood before them.

In a voice that was horribly kind, Wu Fang said, "Good evening, my friends. This is indeed a great pleasure. We have come at last to the final reckoning."

He walked across the floor of the cabin to a narrow little stand. There he placed the small box that he had brought with him. He pointed to it now with a talon-like finger.

"You are perhaps wondering what this box contains," he said. "I will tell you. It contains three of my choicest little death beasts. You are held captive by the paralyzing drug in which the darts which pierced your skin were dipped. You will notice the clock on the front of the box. It will serve two purposes. First, it will help you to watch the few remaining minutes of your life pass by, and, it will also, when the time comes, spring open the lid of the box and release my three little pets. One for each of you. Mohra, my little flower, has arranged everything so that your end will come at the time I have set. She visited each of you less than an hour ago."

Hazard glared at him, but he was powerless to move. Wu Fang chuckled.

"Yes," he said, "she came to you, Mr. Hazard. You thought she was sincere in her actions toward you, but tonight she has doomed you all to death. She has rubbed a sufficient quantity of a certain liquid I have developed which attracts my little beasts much as catnip attracts feline animals. When the clock reaches the prescribed time, the lid of the box will fly open, and my little death beasts will advance upon you, drawn irresistibly by the scent which appeals to them."

The yellow fiend bowed low and strode toward the door of the cabin. There he paused and bowed again.

"I may assure you, my friends," he said, "that the end will not be a pleasant one. It will be the most horribly painful death that it has been my good fortune to invent. While you are being tortured, you may think of me and the yellow mask. It shall be mine, and the yellow race will be dominant in the world. I, Wu Fang, shall be the ruler of all."

With that, he withdrew. The door boomed hollowly behind him.

CHAPTER 16
TORTURE AGENTS

THE DULL boom of the door was like a great gong, sealing their doom. Wu Fang had taken particular pains to switch off the lights, leaving them in darkness.

Although Hazard, like the others, was still paralyzed by the drug, his brain was doubly keen and filled with a tumult of thought. He could hear footsteps padding along the deck. Once, twice, he caught the sound of voices on deck.

There was one sound that came to him, however, more ominous than any he had ever heard in his life. That was the busy clicking of the clock in the box of death as it ticked off the seconds toward their doom. It seemed that it hurried faster and faster as the radium hands moved slowly around the gleaming face of the clock.

It was the only sound that came to him through the inky blackness. If only Wu Fang had told them what time the lid would open! But the yellow fiend had known that the uncertainty would add to their torture, and so he had not told them. They could do nothing except sit or lie there in their rigid positions and wait for the moment when the lid would fly open.

This was indeed the end. Wu Fang had won.

Tick, tock! Tick, tock! Tick, tock! Tick, tock! Tick, tock!

The sound of the clock was driving Hazard insane. Here they were, three of them, all locked up in the cabin, sitting or lying close to each other in the darkness, waiting helplessly for an agonizing death. Perhaps they were even touching each other, but they had no sense of feeling to tell them if they were. They had been robbed of the power of speech. They were as far apart as though they were separated by thousands of miles.

Tick, tock! Tick, tock! Tick, tock!

Hazard's staring eyes saw that the clock had moved five minutes. Another five and it would be one o'clock. Horror seized him. One o'clock. Probably that was the time set for the opening of the cover.

Suddenly, Hazard sensed a change in the rumble of the ship's motors. He was sure they were slowing down. Yes, now they had shut off completely. The freighter must be drifting. He heard the sound of creaking pulleys and hinges. Everything became deathly still, all but the incessant ticking of the clock.

The minute hand pointed to one minute to one. All too rapidly it crossed the half-minute mark. Hazard was frantically sure, now, that the lid of the box would open at one.

To all appearances the ship had been deserted. The motors were stilled and they were drifting, alone, with the bodies of the dead crew lying about the decks. Wu Fang and his agents had escaped, permanently. That didn't matter to Hazard, though, except for the fact that Mohra was with them.

Tick, tock! Tick, tock! Tick, tock!

The minute hand seemed to leap toward the stroke of one. Now it was right on one and moving past. Hazard gasped. Apparently, that wasn't the hour Wu Fang had set for their death, after all. He almost hoped the lid had opened at one o'clock. Anything to end this unbearable suspense.

Tick, tock! Tick, tock! Tick, tock!

Ten minutes after one. Fifteen. Hazard's numbed nerves were at the breaking point. His brain spun with the horrible suspense. Twenty minutes past one.

Tick, tock! Tick, tock! Tick, tock!

Snap!

It was still pitch dark. But the snap meant only one thing to Hazard; the lid of the death box had sprung open. He heard the scraping sound of tiny feet scrambling out of the box; heard a thud. He was sure one of the little death beasts had dropped to the floor of the cabin. Another moment, now, and it would be upon him.

He was suddenly thankful for the paralyzing drug. He wouldn't be able to feel any pain, if those tiny death beasts spread their poison into his body. Not unless—

Another ghastly realization came to him. A prickling sensation in his body told him the effect of the drug was wearing off.

Another of the beasts dropped to the floor now, and then the third came. He could hear them running about, scampering like small rats. There was also a gentle scraping sound. Probably their tails dragging on the floor, he decided. Any moment they would be upon him. Perhaps they were at Kildare and Cappy already.

He felt some bit of life in his fingers and toes, although his arms hung limply at his sides. The trunk of his body also knew the surge of returning strength.

Suddenly, he jerked convulsively as one of the tiny beasts ran up his trouser leg. He tensed for the final blow that would end his life.

AGAIN HE heard a thud. The little beast that had been up his leg had dropped off on the floor again. Strange. He hadn't felt the animal bite or sting him. He moved his arm slowly, tried to get up. If only his feelings and those of the others would return; before the death beasts struck with their poison bite, they might stand a chance.

He heard a scampering just before him on the floor, but the inky darkness prevented him from seeing the beasts. He felt the tiny feet again upon his knee. An appalling sensation flooded over Hazard, driving him half mad as the creature wavered there, digging its little claws into his clothing.

He was sure that any moment would be his last. And Mohra was to blame! She had asked them to trust her, and then she had betrayed them. She had willingly let him hold her close, but that had been only part of the game so she could caress his face and neck with her hands and anoint him with the substance that would attract these demons.

In Hazard's torment, he found himself laughing hysterical-ly—aloud. The paralysis had left his throat now. Suddenly, he checked himself. No, that couldn't be true. Mohra had asked him to trust her and he would, no matter what happened.

He lifted his right arm with an agonizing effort and struck at one of the creatures perched on his knee. It vanished before he touched it. His muscles reacted all too slowly. Yet, he finally managed to gain his feet.

Kildare was mumbling now through a thick tongue, "Hazard! Cappy!"

Cappy tried to answer but could only mutter indistinctly.

As Hazard staggered about the room, he heard the scamper of tiny beasts again. He struggled forward, his strength returning faster and faster. He managed to find the light switch and snap it on.

The light blinded him for a moment. As his eyes became accustomed to it, he saw Kildare and Cappy struggling to their feet. The three little beasts still scampered about on the floor. Horrible little things they were, with tiny feet and rodent's claws. Their tails were what drew Hazard's attention, and he guessed instantly that in them rested the ghastly poison. They were heavy and armored like the tails of tropical lizards, and as long as the whole length of the rest of the body. They ended in sharp, barbed things that reminded Hazard of hypodermic needles.

As he stared, he saw one of the beasts run off Kildare's leg and another leap from Cappy's body. They gave the appearance of fright, as though something about the three men was repulsive to them.

Kildare was on his feet now, staring about for some sort of weapon. He clutched the small ladder that was used for climbing into an upper berth. His actions were apparently difficult as he brought it down toward the place where the little beasts crouched in a corner.

Hazard leaped forward with a cry. "Let me take it, Kildare," he said. "I think I can do it."

He snatched the short ladder from Kildare's hands and jammed the legs down. There was a squeak as the animal was crushed in the middle. Again the newspaperman raised the ladder and struck. This time a spray of colorless liquid came from the sharp barb at the end of the tail.

"Don't let it touch you," Kildare cried out.

Hazard had already leaped back. The two remaining beasts had sprung at him now, and before he could get away, they were on his right leg and crawling up. Suddenly, they dropped to the floor again as though there was something about him that they feared.

Hazard struck again and crushed one body to a pulp. He jammed the legs of the short ladder down once more and killed the other.

Cappy was on his feet, staggering toward Hazard. "Smoke!" he shouted. "I smell smoke!"

Hazard could smell it too. Through the window, he saw a flicker of flame dart from the after part of the freighter.

Kildare hurled himself at the door and Hazard leaped to his aid. The two men stepped back from the door with their shoulders hunched forward.

"One, two, three," counted Kildare, and they charged. The door bulged but snapped back in place again.

"The windows!" Hazard cried. "Maybe we can—" He stopped short. The windows were entirely too small for them to climb through.

Kildare had already sprung for a window and had thrown it open. He jerked his head to Cappy.

"Come on," he said, "you can get out of here, son."

"I think so," said Cappy.

They boosted him through the window and saw him drop to the deck.

"**COME ON,**" Kildare said. "We'll try the door again. It opens from the other side, and that's what makes it so hard to budge." Again and again, they charged the heavy door. Still it held.

Then Hazard heard Cappy's voice from outside the window. "Wait a minute," it said. "I know where there's an ax. It's back on the after deck."

Hazard stared out the window in horror.

"That after deck's a sheet of flame," he yelled. "Don't go back there."

There was no reply from Cappy.

"Come on, we'll try the door again," Hazard yelled. "We can't let the boy burn to death."

Once more they made a frantic effort to break it down, but though it weakened a little, it still held them prisoner.

Then they heard the sound of running feet on deck and Cappy was shouting, "I got it. Wait a minute and I'll break down the door from the outside. Step back so I don't hit you."

Kildare and Hazard moved back, panting as they waited for Cappy to break down the door. A few blows with the ax and the lock flew apart.

"Come on," Cappy yelled. "The whole ship will be on fire in a minute."

"We're free on a burning ship," Hazard yelled as they rushed out on deck. "Where do we go from here, Kildare?"

The government man was at the rail, staring across the waters of the southern Pacific. He pointed, and Hazard saw the lights of a town glowing against the clouds.

"We're going to Peru," Kildare told him. "That's where Wu Fang has gone."

They whirled and looked for a lifeboat that could be used for their escape. Sadly their eyes fell upon the only lifeboat left on board. It was a mass of flames.

"We'll have to swim it," Kildare yelled. Then he raced back to the captain's cabin, returning with three life preservers. He tossed one to Hazard and held one for Cappy.

"Come on, son," he said. "Climb in quickly. The flames are coming this way."

Hazard donned his life preserver and fastened it securely.

"I can swim," he said, "but I'm not much on diving the twenty-odd feet into the water."

"Nor I," Kildare said. "Wait. Here's one of the lowering ropes of the lifeboat that Wu Fang and his agents used. Let's go down on that."

He lifted Cappy over the rail and let him slide down the rope. He waited until Hazard had followed the boy. Then, after taking one last look at the flaming ship, he slid down himself. The water was chilly as they sank into it and began their swim to the far distant shore.

"Take it easy," Kildare advised. "We want to get there as

quickly as possible, but exhaustion won't help us any. I'm praying there aren't any sharks in the water."

CHAPTER 17
DEATH AT THE MICROPHONE

I T WAS high noon when they staggered up a little beach after twelve grueling hours in the water, and fell panting on the blistering hot sands under the merciless sun.

It was apparent to all that Mohra had saved their life, for as Wu Fang had told them, she had been sent to anoint them with a liquid that would attract the death beasts. Had she done that, the beasts would have rushed for them and struck at them with the death-dealing barbs on the ends of the tails the moment they were released from the box. It was apparent, then, that the girl had anointed them not with the attracting fluid but with a substance that gave off an odor repulsive to the animals.

Late that afternoon, they arrived by way of ox-cart and car at Lima, the capital city of Peru. At once they sought the palace of President Fierez. They told his secretary their mission, and were ushered into the presence of the president himself.

President Fierez was a large, plump, genial man, dark-skinned and swarthy. His eyes clouded quickly as Kildare explained their mission.

"We must prevent Wu Fang from finding this yellow golden mask," he told the president. "You know the story concerning the mask, Mr. President?"

"*Si,* senor," Fierez nodded. "The story of Unga and his golden mask is well known here."

"It is true then?" Kildare asked.

"It is based," President Fierez said, "on at least one thing that we know is true, although no one has ever been able to duplicate its power from the insect glands."

He passed his cigars to Kildare and supplied Hazard with a cigarette. Kildare puffed luxuriously.

"The insect glands?" he demanded.

"Yes," President Fierez confirmed. "We have an insect, throughout this section of South America, known as the Cerrosa beetle. It is a most interesting insect. I have often wished that I might be able to make my living in as easy a fashion."

Kildare puffed again on his cigar and sprayed a cloud of smoke from his lips, waiting for the president to go on.

"The Cerrosa beetle is not a fighting insect," the president said, "although it is equipped with very good fighting claws. It preys on other insects in a strange fashion. If you had the powers of the Cerrosa beetle, gentlemen, you would be able to see, let us say, a deer that you desired for food. You would immediately proceed to hypnotize the animal. At first, it would try to draw away. Then it would move in circles ever nearer you. At last it would come directly up to you so that you would have nothing to do but kill it. That's the way in which the Cerrosa beetle works. It hypnotizes other insects, drawing them to it with its irresistible power. Then its ugly claws reach out and strike for the kill."

"Good Lord." Hazard shuddered. "You mean it's as easy as that, President Fierez?"

The president nodded. "I have seen it demonstrated a number of times. Of course, the Cerrosa beetle is not common in South America, although there is evidence that at the time of Unga, there were great numbers of the beetle here."

"But what," Kildare demanded, "has that got to do with the golden mask of Unga?"

The president puffed at his cigar and crossed one heavy leg over the other before he answered.

"The legend has it that there's a certain part of the Cerrosa beetle, a very small gland, which produces a secretion that if rubbed around the eyes of a human being will give him or her strange powers of hypnotism that no other human being can resist."

"Has anyone ever proved this statement?" Kildare asked.

President Fierez shook his head. "Not to my knowledge. Our university here in Lima has worked upon the subject and has made many experiments with the Cerrosa beetle, to no avail. It is commonly thought that the legend of the golden mask is purely folklore built around the fact that Unga was supposed to control his subjects in a manner similar to the hypnotism of the Cerrosa beetle."

"Then," said Kildare, "you believe Wu Fang came down here on a wild goose chase?"

"You mean," asked President Fierez, a puzzled frown on his face, "that he has wasted his time in coming here to search for the yellow mask?"

Kildare nodded assent.

"I would say so," said the president, "but on the other hand, we are not certain and it is, of course, to the advantage of all the white people in the world that this yellow maniac be stopped as soon as possible." He glanced at his watch.

"I am due to deliver a message over the air at seven o'clock from our powerful Lima radio station. They tell me that every citizen in Peru who can get to a radio will be there listening to my talk. I will tell them of Wu Fang's arrival into this country with his agents, and I will ask for help from all corners of Peru, particularly, in the region of Tiahuanaco. That, you know, is where the center of Unga's civilization was located. There are many great cavernous temples and ruins of buildings near Tiahuanaco. A map was discovered on the wall of a temple a few days ago by a scientist. It purported to tell where the sacred mask of Unga is hidden. I have a copy of that map that I can show you, if you like. Will you have dinner with me? Afterwards, we will come back here for the radio broadcast, at seven o'clock. Will that be satisfactory, senors?"

"Perfectly," nodded Kildare. "I would like very much to see a copy of that map."

"There is a strange happening connected with its discovery," President Fierez told him. "The scientist who discovered it less than two weeks ago—his name was Combardo—died the night he brought the copy to my residence. They found him out near the gate of the estate.

The cause of his death has not been determined, as yet, but the doctors suspect poison. Although they cannot find any evidence of it in his body. But come. We'll see the map that I have mentioned. It is in my vault in the cellar."

LEAVING THE president's office, they were met by three of his secretaries, hurrying up a great, spacious hallway. The president addressed them in rapid Spanish, apparently questioning them. Kildare and Hazard could not understand what they were saying, but they could see the president become excited. Suddenly, he started on a half run.

"I must ask your indulgence," he called over his shoulder, "but something terrible has happened. My secretaries report that the guard of the vault has been found dead before its open doors. We go there at once, senors."

They followed the president and his secretaries down winding flights to the great, dark cellar below the presidential mansion. They found themselves staring at the body of a man on the floor, dressed in the uniform of a Peruvian guard.

Kildare bent over him, searched the back of his neck and throat, stroked the hair at the back of his head.

"Here it is," he said. "A dart mark. See it?"

The president nodded.

"*Si*, senor," he said. "You think that is the cause of his death?"

"I am positive of it," Kildare assured him.

They rose, turning toward the open door of the vault. President Fierez uttered a cry of dismay and leaped forward.

"*Sacre dieu!*" he cried. "There is nothing in the vault! My gold, it is gone!"

"And the copy of the map, was that here, too?" Kildare demanded.

172

"*Si*, senor," the president groaned, "that is gone, too. This is terrible. I do not know how such a thing could happen."

"Are there any secret passages leading out of this cellar?" Kildare demanded.

The president stood stock still, staring hard at Kildare. He turned suddenly and dismissed his secretaries. As they were leaving, he said loudly, "No, no, senor. There is no passage leading out of the cellar."

But the moment his secretaries were out of hearing he added hoarsely, "I hope I can trust you, senors."

"You may absolutely," Kildare assured him.

President Fierez continued in low voice, "I will tell you the truth. There is a strong faction here in Peru against me. I have been afraid of revolutions, of being captured, perhaps by the enemy. When I took office and moved into the palace, I had a few of my friends secretly build me a passage out of the cellar."

"In that case," Kildare said, "it would be as easy for someone to get into this place from outside as it would be for you to escape from within, provided, of course, that they knew where the passage was."

Fierez nodded slowly. "Yes," he said, "I am afraid that is true."

"Will you show us the entrance to the passage from the cellar?"

"*Si*, senor."

The president turned and led the way down a dimly-lighted corridor to the west wing of the palace. They left the corridor there and entered a small room, obviously used for storage purposes. The president stopped and peered through the dimness.

"Sacre dieu!" he exclaimed again in dismay. "Someone has come through the secret passage."

A heavy bolt was bent where the door had been forced open by some instrument. Kildare entered the passage and lit a match. He held the flame close to the dusty floor, examining.

"See, Jerry?"

As Hazard bent down beside him, he saw the imprint of a bare foot in the dust.

"I believe," said Kildare, turning to the president, "if I were in your place, I would have a guard stationed here."

At that suggestion, the president's face went a little white.

"But, senor," he protested, "this is a secret passage."

"Apparently," Kildare observed, "it isn't as secret as it might be."

"Yes, I guess you are right," President Fierez admitted. "I will see to it. Come, we must go upstairs now. It is nearly time to eat. Then I speak over the radio to my countrymen."

The president ordered suitable clothing for them. Dinner was an impressive affair, but it was apparent that President Fierez wasn't enjoying it. His mind was still on the discovery of the secret passage and on the disappearance of the map and his gold.

At length, he nodded. "You will pardon me, senors," he said, "but it is nearly time for my radio talk. You will come with me?"

"By all means," Kildare nodded.

"Gladly," agreed Hazard.

Returning, they found the president's personal secretary in

the study. As they entered, he laid out the speech and adjusted a desk microphone for the president's convenience.

"As a matter of precaution," Kildare suggested, "would you happen to have some pistols you could loan us? And, perhaps, some flashlights would not be amiss."

A frightened look came into the president's eyes.

"Surely you do not expect trouble here during the broadcast?" he asked.

"You never can tell," Kildare said with a shrug. "I certainly hope not."

PRESIDENT FIEREZ spoke to his personal secretary in Spanish, and the other went out. A moment later, the guns and flashes were provided.

Hazard surveyed the room with interest as he waited for orders from Kildare. There was only darkness outside.

The president glanced at his watch and nodded to his secretary, who leaned over the microphone from the opposite side of the desk and spoke in Spanish. When the secretary had finished, the president bent down slightly and began to talk.

Hazard knew enough Spanish to pick up parts of the speech but he couldn't get it all. However, he knew that the speech began with the affairs of state.

Then the president hesitated and cleared his throat. Hazard heard him say in Spanish, "And now we come to a crisis that has just arisen in Peru." He rattled on. Hazard couldn't understand anything he said until he heard him mention Wu Fang.

There was a sound of crashing glass, and as Kildare whirled, he saw a figure at the window. His gun barked twice and there was a scream, a horrible scream that made the shivers run up and down Hazard's back. He turned in time to see a ghastly figure topple from the ledge.

The two men whirled and stared at Fierez. The president of Peru had pitched forward on his desk, and there was a tiny mark of blood on the left side of the neck, where a small dart still protruded.

CHAPTER 18
A STOLEN CORPSE

KILDARE SPUN around to the secretary who spoke English. "Quick!" he barked. "Get on that microphone. Tell the people of Peru that Wu Fang and his agents are abroad, that they're probably in Tiahaunaco right now, and that they'll kill everyone in Peru rather than leave a stone unturned in their search for the golden mask of Unga."

For an instant, the secretary's face was a mask of frozen horror. He stared blankly at the prostrate form of the president. Then, with an effort, he rose to the occasion, stepped to the microphone, and began speaking rapidly in Spanish. As he closed, he gave orders that any of the police, national army men, or citizens who happened to come in contact with Wu Fang and his agents should telephone the president's palace at once.

Kildare, Hazard, Cappy, and the secretary rushed out into the hall and out of doors. The secretary explained their presence to the guards who challenged them. Then he turned to Kildare.

"He says they have found the body of the man you shot," he

said. "The captain of the guard commends you, senor, for your excellent shooting. There was a bullet through his head."

"We'll have a look at him," Kildare said.

Hazard shuddered as he looked upon the dead figure of the man on the ground.

"He's like other agents of Wu Fang that I have seen," Kildare observed. "They come from a strange tribe of Malayans that live near the Chinese border. They are extremely skillful in the use of a blow pipe. We've seen evidence of that before. Do you smell the odor that exudes from his body?"

Hazard nodded, wrinkling his nose in distaste. "How could anybody miss it?" he asked.

"It's one of their beliefs," Kildare explained, "that they are damned if they ever bathe. But strangely enough, they are a very intelligent group of people. It's their fantastic religion that keeps them down. I hadn't known of Wu Fang's using these men until we began working on this case."

He turned to the secretary, "You may as well have the guards move him away," he said.

"And what will we do with President Fierez?" the other asked. "Should we tell the people of Peru that he is dead?"

Kildare shook his head. "Not yet," he advised. "Better wait a while."

Hazard easily guessed the reason for Kildare's advice. If the public learned suddenly that President Fierez had been killed, the revolution that he had feared so, might break out.

"I think," Kildare said, "it would be best to have President

Fierez's body removed to his bedroom. If anyone asks the cause of his breaking off so abruptly, tell them he had a fainting spell."

"*Si*, senor," nodded the secretary.

"What do we do now?" Hazard asked Kildare.

"At least for a few minutes," Kildare said, "I think we had better go back into the president's study and wait for any calls that might come in. Then we'll be on our way."

The first secretary accompanied them into the study to wait for any late news.

"We've got one of these blowers," Kildare said as he sat down, "but you had better sit facing the window in case there might be more of them about."

They sat for some time, smoking. At length, the telephone rang.

"You answer it," Kildare said, jerking his head to the secretary. "I can't speak Spanish."

The secretary picked up the receiver and spoke at some length.

"It is word from Tiahuanaco," he said. "The chief of police there has called to tell us that this morning a party answering the description of your Chinese friend and his agents left for the ruins. They have sent word ahead into the jungle to an army garrison to apprehend them as soon as possible. The soldiers will take care of them, senor. You can depend on that."

Kildare shrugged. "Perhaps," he said. "Anyway, let's hope they're successful." He walked to the president's desk, picked up a pocketful of cigars, and turned toward the door.

"Let's go," he said. "We're on their trail, at least."

In the hall, they heard the sound of running feet from the

floor above. The president's second secretary was plunging down the steps, babbling excitedly. He was followed by a dark man with a close-cropped beard whom, as yet, they hadn't seen.

The first secretary listened to the other for a moment. He turned quickly and explained, "Something terrible has happened. The president's second secretary tells me they took the body of President Fierez into his bedroom and placed it on his bed. Then Doctor Madriguera, the president's physician, was summoned. When they returned, the president's body had vanished! They can find no trace of him anywhere!"

"Come on," Kildare shouted. "Show me where his room is."

The secretary pointed to an open door off the head of the stairs. Kildare lunged in, Hazard and Cappy on his heels.

Hazard glanced about and saw that the bed where the president had lain was mussed, but aside from that, the room seemed quite orderly.

Kildare was at one of the windows, examining it.

"Forced," he said tersely.

He threw up the sash. In the light of his electric torch he examined the sill.

"Jerry," he said, "look here."

Hazard ran to the open window and stared out. A knotted rope hung from the ledge.

"Whoever it was that stole the president's body got away down this rope," Kildare said. He turned to the first secretary. "QUICK! HAVE the guards and the whole army search the entire estate at once. This is the worst thing that has happened yet. Don't give up the search until you have found the president.

Have the entire city of Lima surrounded as soon as it can be done."

Kildare turned and ran into the hall and down the stairs, still shouting orders to the secretary.

"Get on that phone," the government man cried, "and broadcast these orders over the air."

At the door, he stopped. He jerked his head toward the outside.

"Come on," he said to Hazard and Cappy. "We're starting for Tiahuanaco at once."

On the train, Hazard spoke.

"I can't figure it out, Kildare. What earthly good would the body of President Fierez do Wu Fang?"

Kildare smiled.

"I was afraid you didn't get it, Jerry, and I'm not going to help you out a great deal. I may be wrong in my suspicions, you know. If I am, there's no need of you and the whole Peruvian citizenry worrying yourselves sick about it. But I will say this. I don't believe that the President's dead body was stolen from his bedroom."

Jerry Hazard stared, scarcely believing his ears.

"What did you say, Kildare?" he asked.

"I said," Kildare repeated, "that I don't believe it was President Fierez's dead body Wu Fang's agents stole from his bedroom."

"Good Lord, Kildare," Hazard exploded. "Are you crazy?"

"Perhaps." Kildare laughed. "I'll leave it up to you to decide. If you can't figure it out, then you will simply have to wait and see how my theory develops. I think my berth is made up, so I'm going to turn in."

Jerry Hazard got little sleep that night. Over and over in his mind he kept turning the events which puzzled him. Then, as always, his thoughts drifted to Mohra, and he fell asleep thinking of her.

It seemed to him that he had barely closed his eyes when he heard Kildare shouting in his ear—

"Get up. We're coming into Tiahuanaco."

When they reached police headquarters in Tiahuanaco, they found an interpreter was necessary, since no one present spoke English.

The first question that Hazard asked when they had procured one was, "Did you see a woman in the party that you suspected?"

"*Si,* senor," the chief of police answered. "There was a very beautiful woman."

Hazard could hardly conceal his impatience as a jungle party was made up that morning to start for the ruins. They traveled first by car and then by pack train over the rough trail. It was nearly dark when they reached the first of the ruins. The interpreter, as well as the rest of the natives in the party, was plainly nervous.

"My countrymen," the interpreter explained, "say that it would be best to camp here and wait until tomorrow to go into the temple where the map of the golden mask was discovered."

Kildare hesitated. He pointed to a long, lean Peruvian guide, standing near the lead horse of the pack train.

"He is the one who was with Combardo, the scientist, when he uncovered the map on the wall of the temple, isn't he?"

"*Si*, senor," the interpreter answered. "He is Carlos, the one who has been in the temple before, but he also thinks it best that we camp here."

"Call him over," Kildare ordered.

At the interpreter's command, the man came over.

"Ask him how far that temple is from here," Kildare ordered.

There was an exchange of words between the guide and the interpreter. Then the latter turned to Kildare.

"He says that the temple is a little over two miles from here. It will be an easy journey in the morning."

Kildare's jaw was firmly set as he said, "We will make it tonight. It will be dark inside the temple anyway in the daytime. There is no time to lose."

Grudgingly, the Peruvians moved on. Great trees overhung the rough path that had been cut through the jungle for them, shutting out the rapidly failing daylight. Twice, Hazard drew back as a great snake lowered from a branch. Then his automatic spat flame and the snake writhed convulsively and fell to the ground, almost striking him with its falling body. Strange insects hummed about. Hazard began to wish they had taken the advice of the Peruvian natives and pitched camp as suggested.

It was dark when they reached the newly uncovered temple of Unga, and they could see only by the light of their electric torches.

"Carlos will guide you to where you may see the map," the interpreter told Kildare. "We will wait outside."

Hazard knew the Peruvian natives had made up their minds not to enter the temple after dark.

"Let's go in," Kildare suggested. "We'll have a look at that map and then push on."

THEIR LIGHT reflected eerily as they descended the few steps into the ghostly interior of the great temple. Kildare stopped. He bent over to examine the floor.

"Look," he said. "Here's marks of bare feet and—"

He stopped short, and Hazard saw his finger point now, to another long, narrow footprint. As Kildare spoke again, his voice was husky and low.

"Wu Fang stepped there," he said, "not so long ago."

Their lights showed Carlos ahead, walking toward a wall at the side of the great vaulted interior in a small recess behind a heavily carved stone rostrum. There he stopped and pointed silently to the wall itself.

Hazard saw a strange map. A line ran up it, indicating a trail, terminated by a crude picture of a bird. Then there was what seemed to be a vine, running from that to the right. Farther up on the wall at the end of the line there was a circle. From this there were marks, not unlike a child's drawing of the sun. Under the circle, a jagged line extended across the map, as though the sun were rising or setting. Below this strange map was another drawing resembling the floor plan of a building. One entrance to the nearly square room was pictured there, and in the center of it was a rectangle. A crude drawing of a mask was scratched on the rock at the end of this rectangle, surrounded by a square outline.

Kildare jerked his head toward the entrance and Carlos led them out.

"Have Carlos explain the map to us," Kildare ordered the interpreter, who met them outside.

The interpreter spoke to Carlos, who answered at great length in Spanish.

"He says," the interpreter explained, "that the line running up the wall with the vines at the end of it and the sun above, on a jagged line, mean we should take a trail directly to the east if we wish to find the golden mask."

"You mean," demanded Kildare, "that he's taking for granted that the sun is rising?"

"He says there are jagged mountains to the east that begin from the bottom of the cliffs and go straight up. To the west you see no mountains. That is the reason for the jagged line under the sun. That tells that the sun is rising over the mountains and in that way Carlos knows it is east, senor. There are many large birds nesting in the cliffs, and great vines hang down over them."

"And the other drawing of a room?" Kildare probed.

"That," said the interpreter, "is believed to be the tomb of Unga. It is hidden at the point where the great vines come down over the cliff."

"How is it," Kildare demanded, "that this tomb of Unga wasn't uncovered as soon as they found the map and deciphered it?"

"Because," the interpreter explained, "we Peruvians have a superstition that whoever uncovers the tomb of Unga will be cursed with bad luck for the rest of his life. He will die of strange things."

Carlos spoke again to the interpreter, who turned and said, "I am sorry, senors, but my people refuse to go on tonight to the tomb of Unga. They are afraid."

Kildare hesitated for a moment. Then he nodded.

"All right, we will camp here for the night."

Hazard slept but little that night. He was awakened suddenly toward morning by a sharp cry, a scream such as Captain Malloy had uttered on board the Ocola. Even before it died away in its horribly gurgling sound, he knew what it was. He heard a shot ring out, and as he sat up, he saw Kildare's flash shining on something that fell to the ground.

"I've got it!" Kildare shouted.

CHAPTER 19
THE LASH OF LOVE

HAZARD WAS up in a bound, running toward the edge of the camp where Kildare was headed. He reached the government man's side just as he bent down to pick something up. In the light of the electric torch, Hazard saw it was a mass of feathers, muddy brown feathers, spattered with blood.

The limp bird had a wicked hawk-like beak and staring eyes. Kildare picked up one stout leg and examined the vicious talons.

"Ever see one of these before, Jerry?"

185

"No," Hazard answered. "I've seen birds like it, though. There's a sparrow hawk in America about the same size, isn't there?"

"Yes," Kildare agreed. "This bird, altogether, would measure eight or nine inches in length, I should say, with a fourteen- or fifteen-inch wing spread. But look at the legs and talons."

Hazard stared at them in amazement. The legs and talons seemed all out of proportion to the rest of the bird. It was as though the legs and talons of a much larger hawk, or an eagle, had been grafted onto this bird.

"I encountered one of these once," Kildare said, "in the Gobi Desert. It is known to the explorers as the Gobi Desert night hawk. They attack by tearing out the throat of their victim, as you have already seen. But of course the talons of this particular one have been frequently dipped in poison. That's what has been causing the sudden death of the men it has attacked. I hope they had only one of these creatures, so we'll be safe from at least one menace."

He tossed the remains of the bird back into the jungle, being careful not to let the sharp, needle-like talons touch his flesh as he flung it away.

When they returned to camp, they found a frightened group of people surrounding a still, bloody form on the ground. As Kildare flashed his light on the ground, he saw it was one of his guides, the short, stocky native who had accompanied him.

"You see," Kildare remarked, "he died like the rest. His throat was torn out by the claws. Well"—he shrugged now—"we may as well turn in again and get some sleep if we can."

But Hazard pointed to the eastern sky, where the gray light of dawn was spreading.

"I couldn't get back to sleep if I wanted to," he said, "and besides, it's going to be morning soon."

"That's right," Kildare admitted. "I hadn't realized it."

Most of the camp was awake as Kildare gave the order to prepare for departure. Hazard awakened Cappy while the natives prepared breakfast. After a hurried meal, they started for the tomb of Unga.

They had gone but little over a mile when Carlos halted. He called back to the interpreter.

"Carlos wishes you to come forward," the interpreter explained to Kildare.

Hazard and Cappy rode up with Kildare to where Carlos was pointing at the ground. They saw another narrow trail there that joined the one they were on. They could see many hoof prints as they stared.

"There certainly have been a lot of horses along here lately," Kildare said. "Ask Carlos how long he thinks it has been since they passed."

A moment later the interpreter answered, "Carlos said these horses passed only a few hours ago, probably during the night."

"I wonder what it means," Hazard puzzled.

Kildare shrugged. "I don't know," he said. "I'm afraid we're going to find out, though, and very shortly. Come on. Let's push ahead."

Strange rustlings of animals or humans came to them from the brush beside the trail. Hazard hadn't the slightest doubt

that they were being followed. Any moment a new menace might break out, but he had no idea of what awaited them at the entrance to the tomb of Unga.

Through the trees they began to see great towering cliffs before them. Around a break in the trail, where the jungle

She raised the whip again
with a slow, weird rhythm.

suddenly gave way to an open, flat area, they came upon horses
and men, perhaps seventy-five or a hundred of them.

The men were dressed in the uniforms of Peruvian soldiers.
An armed guard of twelve riders came galloping toward them
as they appeared on the plain.

Hazard grasped for his gun.

"Take it easy," Kildare warned. "We seem to be in trouble, but I don't think fighting will get us out of it. Wait until we find out what it's all about."

He gave orders to the interpreter, who passed them on to the natives. Now they were completely surrounded by the twelve riders. After a long conversation with the leader of the Peruvian guard, the interpreter turned to Kildare.

"We are informed," he said, "that we are under arrest by special order of President Fierez."

"President Fierez!" exploded Hazard.

Kildare groaned. "I was afraid of that."

"But President Fierez is dead!" Hazard cried.

The interpreter shook his head. "Apparently not. They say he is here. They order us to go forward under their guard."

THE PACK train moved on, with mounted soldiers taking up either flank across the plain. They threaded their way through grazing horses and lounging soldiers to the very face of the cliff. There, going up the cliff, they saw a great mass of vines, the stalks as thick around as the trunks of a large tree. Hazard remembered the map on the wall of the temple. There had been a vine there in the days of Unga, and it was undoubtedly the same one now.

Then, as his eyes traveled past the vine and through it, he caught sight of a small opening at the side of the cliff. Apparently it had been made only recently, as there was new dirt spread across the flat lands at the bottom.

Suddenly, Hazard was transfixed with amazement as he saw

a figure standing in that hole at the base of the cliff. He blinked and shook his head and stared again. Yes, it was true. That was President Fierez standing there, hale and hearty as ever. He had just come from the tomb of Unga and was walking toward them.

There was an angry look on his round face as he spoke to Kildare. "Senor Kildare, permit me to inform you that you and your assistants are under arrest."

Hazard stared in amazement at the president of Peru, who had apparently been dead but was now alive and talking to them. Wu Fang must have administered some strange narcotic on him that had given the appearance of death. The yellow fiend had planned to use him later; hence the theft of the body from the bedroom. He was alive, yes; but was he normal?

"You have reported senor Wu Fang," he was saying, "as a most dangerous man. You may be interested to know that he and I have formed an alliance. He is to take possession of the world with the aid of the golden mask of Unga, and I, for my assistance to him, will be commander of all South America. I turn you over now to my commander and ally."

With that, he turned and spoke rapidly in Spanish. In a moment there was a surge of soldiers about the three Americans. Desperately, Hazard groped for his gun.

"Don't do it, Jerry," Kildare snapped. "They'll kill you. Surrender peacefully. It's our only hope."

At the same moment, Hazard's gun was knocked out of his hand and his arm twisted painfully. He was then jerked from his horse. All three of them were pushed toward the opening in the face of the cliff with their arms pinioned behind them. Kildare was thrust in first, then Hazard, then Cappy. Their guns and flashlights were gone. They were stripped of all means of defense.

A dim light glowed within, but Hazard could see nothing. The sun outside had been so bright that the change was too abrupt for him. He knew, however, that shadowy forms were peering out of the darkness.

Strong hands were laid upon him and he felt himself being propelled forward. He couldn't see Cappy and Kildare but he knew they must be coming on, too. As his eyes became accustomed to the dim light inside the tomb of Unga, he saw the rectangular thing that had been marked on the wall. It was a large stone case. In all probability it contained what remained of the great Unga. Then he made out a small square receptacle no bigger than a hat box at the foot of the sarcophagus. The top of it was off and it was completely empty. That meant but one thing. The golden mask of Unga, which had reposed in that box for a thousand years or more, was gone.

A familiar figure appeared suddenly in front of them. The yellow silk robe, sloping shoulders, high forehead, and long face of Wu Fang were all too well known to the three Americans. He faced them with his characteristically mocking smile on his thin, cruel lips. In his hand he held the golden mask of Unga.

"It is a pleasure to be together, my friends," he said with a bow. "I thought for a time that our enmity had ceased in the captain's cabin on the Ocola, but it seems that was not to be. My little flower, Mohra, I have learned, took pity on you and anointed you with the odor that repelled my little beasts. However, that can be easily remedied."

He smiled again as he addressed his speech to Hazard.

"Mohra, my beautiful one," he said, "will inflict punishment upon you almost as great as that which I had planned with my little beasts. We will begin at once."

The yellow fiend pointed to the low ceiling of the tomb, and Hazard saw a crudely-carved rock ledge jutting out a few feet above their heads.

"You will hang Mr. Hazard by his hands," he ordered his agents, "from that ledge up there."

Hazard stared up at the jutting rock in horror. If that rock broke—and it appeared none too safe—it would crush him when it fell. Yet, perhaps it would be the easiest way out.

Strong brown hands raised his arms above his head and tied them securely by the wrists. He suddenly found himself jerked from his feet, hanging there from the rock ledge. Already the bindings hurt his wrists as his whole weight was suspended from them.

Now he saw Kildare and Cappy being tied close by him against rocks that jutted similarly. Wu Fang stood back, directing the whole procedure, smiling cruelly.

Suddenly, he said softly, "Mohra, you may come now."

Hazard's eyes bulged as they stared at Wu Fang. The gleaming yellow mask was raised before the glowing green eyes of the Dragon Lord of Crime, with his left hand, and with his right he was pointing ahead, fingers outstretched, in the manner of a hypnotist.

The newspaperman turned quickly as he heard a sound behind him. His heart leaped. Mohra was walking toward him.

She came as though she were asleep. There was no sign of recognition in her face as she stopped in front of him. She wore a simple blue sport dress. She had something in her hand. At first, Hazard thought it was a snake, but he saw now that it was a long whip with torturing barbs on the end of the lash.

"WE ARE ready to have Mr. Hazard stripped for the ceremony," Wu Fang said. He raised his hand a little now, so that it was on a level with Mohra's eyes as she stood there staring fixedly at him.

"Mohra, Mohra!" Hazard cried. "Don't you know me? I'm Jerry. Jerry Hazard. Look at me."

The girl turned slowly with her lovely eyes upon him but still gave no evidence of seeing him. Wu Fang uttered a command, and the girl's lithe body swayed as she raised the whip. The lash circled Hazard's body, and cracked down. The barbs dug into his flesh. There was no need of looking down. He knew that the first blow had brought blood. She raised the whip again and brought it down again, and again, with a slow, weird rhythm.

Crack! Crack! Crack!

Jerry Hazard's body writhed under the pain of the assault. He felt the blood oozing from the wounds and trickling down his back.

Crack! Crack! Crack!

The lashing continued, mercilessly, as Wu Fang looked on with gloating eyes.

"Mohra, Mohra!" Hazard yelled at the top of his voice. "Don't you know me? You're whipping me. Me, Jerry Hazard. Mohra!"

The pain had become almost unbearable. Still the girl kept on, relentlessly. Her movements were like those of a machine rather than of a human being.

Crack! Crack! Crack!

At the same time, Hazard heard Kildare cry out, "Back you devils, back!"

He and Cappy were bound against the wall not far from him. Two ghastly-looking snakes were wriggling and writhing from the edge of the overhanging rocks above him. Any moment they would strike.

Crack! Crack! Crack!

To Hazard the pain of seeing Mohra there, lashing him under Wu Fang's power, was even greater than the physical torment. He could hardly see her now, for his vision was blurred with the perspiration agony had wrung from his body.

Suddenly, through the fog of torture, he heard other sounds above the crack of the whip. There was shouting and yelling from outside the tomb. He heard a gun bark. He saw dimly that Wu Fang had turned and was running toward the entrance of the tomb. Then came the pounding of running feet as the agents of Wu Fang followed him through the opening, into the clear morning air.

The sudden uproar had its effect on Mohra. The movement of her whip slowed, and Hazard felt the strength had left her blows.

Suddenly the girl stopped altogether, and a choked sob left

her lips. She stood there for a moment with the lash in her hand, staring wild-eyed at Hazard. She cried out.

"Jerry, Jerry," she choked, "I didn't know. I—"

Hazard jerked his head around and stared at Cappy and Kildare. The snakes had advanced slowly toward them but as yet had not struck.

"Quick, Mohra!" Hazard cried in alarm. "Those snakes!"

Mohra turned her lovely head and a horrified expression came into her eyes. She leaped forward with the whip upraised. The heavy lash whistled through the air.

Again Mohra lashed her whip and struck with all her might at the serpent before Kildare. There was a hissing sound as the snake struck at Kildare's face, but the lash, with the other snake still tangled up in it, struck a split second sooner.

Mohra was beating the snakes' heads into a pulp with the handle of her whip. Next, she whirled and came back to Hazard.

"Jerry, Jerry," she said, "I've hurt you horribly." As she spoke, she was standing on tiptoe, trying to reach the ropes that bound him.

"There's a jackknife in my pocket," Hazard gasped.

In an instant Mohra had the knife out. She jumped until she caught the rope with one hand and hung beside him. She slashed the rope with one hand, and they dropped together in a little heap.

Mohra was helping Hazard to his feet. He was so weak he could hardly stand.

"Quick, Mohra," he said. "Get Cappy and Kildare loose."

The girl ran to where they were bound and began cutting

them down with Hazard's knife. Cappy fell to his knees as the ropes gave way, and Mohra was in back of Kildare, cutting the ropes that bound him.

Meanwhile, the cracking and blasting of gunfire outside the tomb had continued. A deafening roar came to their ears, apparently from overhead, opposite the entrance to the tomb.

As the roar increased in sound, Hazard started toward it. Kildare staggered up to him and caught his arm.

"For the love of heaven," the government man said, "don't go out there."

As he spoke, Hazard saw the daylight shining through the small opening suddenly disappear, and, as the roaring ended with a thunderous crash, they found themselves shut in, as if a heavy door had been slammed in front of the entrance.

Then, Hazard heard Kildare's voice echo hollowly against the walls of the tomb. "We're trapped in here!"

CHAPTER 20
THE GOLDEN MASK

HAZARD REALIZED with a sense of shock that there could be little doubt to what Kildare had said. Nevertheless he staggered toward the entrance to the tomb. He could see great, ghostly bats fluttering eerily about the dark recesses of the tomb. He struck viciously at the winged beasts.

"Something must have started a landslide that covered the mouth of the tomb," Kildare said. "I think there's enough air in here to breathe for quite a long time. But we've got to get out. Wu Fang is gone, and he's got the yellow mask."

In the dim light that still glowed overhead, Hazard saw Mohra coming toward him. She was tearing part of her dress into long strips.

"Jerry," she said as she reached him, "I—I wasn't myself. I hope you know that. I—I—"

Her words were choked off, and he saw her lovely eyes fill with tears as she looked at the great welts on his body. She wound the bandages about him, the soft touch of her fingers more soothing than any remedy that could be applied.

"It's all right, Mohra—darling," Hazard said. "We're together now and we're going to stay together, always. Wu Fang has gone. You've broken clear of him at last."

"What was the power that you felt from that mask, Mohra?" Kildare asked.

"I—I don't know," Mohra choked out, as she continued to bind Hazard's wounds. "I don't remember."

"What I can't understand," Hazard ventured, "is how that hypnotic power of the mask was broken."

"Those things are hard to explain," Kildare said. "Mohra, do you remember anything about the circumstances of the president's being brought back to life, and Wu Fang casting his spell over him?"

The girl nodded. "Yes. That, of course, was one of Wu Fang's tricks. President Fierez was not really dead. He was brought here unconscious by Wu Fang's agents. Narcotics brought him back to life. Then he put on the yellow mask, and with the help of that he made the president agree to do everything he ordered."

"I see," Kildare said, "and in the meantime, the president's special bodyguard had trailed him here."

"Yes," Mohra said, "and then Wu Fang sent President Fierez out with a message to the cavalry that he was now in league with Wu Fang; that they were to do anything Wu Fang ordered."

"Apparently," Kildare said, "the hypnotic spell that Wu Fang cast over you was counteracted by the sudden change that took place when the shooting occurred."

"The only thing I remember," Mohra said, "was that everything seemed to be bursting apart in my head. Then I heard the gunfire. Suddenly, everything seemed to be perfectly normal again. Perhaps—perhaps it was Jerry who helped me. I remember now that somebody seemed to be crying. Suddenly, I realized it was Jerry and that I had been whipping him."

Her voice broke again, but Kildare probed on: "What is the force by which Wu Fang holds you, Mohra?" he asked.

The girl caught her breath quickly before she faltered, "I—I don't know exactly. Just the mention of his name seems to do things to me; but I think I am working away from him gradually. Those green eyes when they glow—I don't think it's real hypnotism because I know everything that goes on all the time. Still, I haven't the power to disobey his orders—unless, it concerns Jerry."

Kildare turned abruptly toward the entrance of the tomb, and Cappy went with him. Mohra laid her hand lightly on Hazard's arm.

"Come," she said, "we've got to help them. We've got to get out of here."

Reluctantly, Jerry Hazard followed her as she led him toward the debris that covered the entrance. At that moment he felt he would be content to stay alone in the tomb with her until they died. But he knew that was no solution. They must go on. Wu Fang was at large with this strange, powerful mask. If he could get to other rulers of countries as he had to President Fierez, his world domination would be sure.

"There's some slabs of rock you can use for shovels," Kildare said as they reached the entrance. "It may be possible that they'll dig us out of here, but we may as well do our share. We might sit here until doomsday waiting for them."

No sound came to them except the slashing of their stone shovels. There was no telling how deep the landslide was at the entrance.

The strain began to tell on Hazard, as he knew it was telling on the others. The exertion of digging was rapidly using up the oxygen inside the tomb. It seemed that he couldn't go on much longer. He was reeling dizzily as he worked.

Suddenly, he heard Kildare gasp, "We've got it! I can see daylight through a couple of rocks ahead. Jerry, come here and give me a hand."

They finally managed to push the rocks aside and crawl out through the opening, choking and gasping as they inhaled the clear air.

A strange sight greeted their eyes as they sank on the ground to rest. A motley crew of natives garbed in the dress of the

Peruvian peasantry and armed with heavy rifles approached them. Behind, they could see soldiers and horses lying dead.

"There has been a revolution," Kildare said. "I wonder if any of these birds speak English."

He called out a question to that effect. A long, slim, bronzed figure with a cartridge belt slung across each shoulder came striding up.

"Well, if it ain't a bunch of Americans," he said in typical Yankee English. "Where the devil did you come from?"

Hazard and the others stared at him in amazement.

THE OTHER laughed. "You don't have to look at me like that. Haven't you ever heard of a soldier of fortune? Well, that's me. Tommy Ryan, at your service, colonel in the Peruvian revolutionary forces. Have you seen anything of President Fierez? You know he's the so-and-so that was going to turn the government over to the yellow devil. Did you hear about it?"

Kildare nodded. He rose, extending his hand to Ryan. The others joined in the handshaking. Hazard introduced Mohra, saying nothing about her connection with Wu Fang.

"We haven't seen anything of President Fierez," Kildare said. "We've been cooped up in the tomb for nearly three hours. Have you seen anything of Wu Fang?"

"Some of my boys that were fighting near here," Ryan said, "told me that they saw a gang of yellow and brown men pouring out of the hole in the cliff."

"Did they catch them?" Kildare cried.

"No," Ryan said, "the fighting was pretty stiff at that time and they must have escaped behind the federal troops."

"We've got to get after them, then," Kildare said. "Can we get some horses around here to take us back to Tiahuanaco?"

"Sure," Ryan said, "and well go back with you. We'll probably be needed ourselves."

Suddenly, Kildare stopped short, staring to the left, near where the slide had ended on the plain. A man's foot protruded from the debris, a little of the trouser leg showing. Below that, a buttoned shoe with a pearl gray top. Kildare turned quickly to Ryan.

"If you're looking for President Fierez," he said, "I think you'll find what remains of him under that pile of stone and dirt. I remember he was wearing shoes like that."

Ryan turned to his men, and they began digging about the body. A few minutes later, they had uncovered the crushed form of President Fierez. As they laid him out on the ground, Ryan looked up at the condors, circling about, waiting for the living men to depart.

"We'll leave him for the condors, I guess," the Yankee said.

But Kildare shook his head. "No," he said, "I would hate to think of that, Ryan. You see, I happen to know that President Fierez wasn't a bad sort of man at heart. The alliance he made with Wu Fang was due to a hypnotic spell that the yellow devil cast over him with the golden mask. I think he deserves a decent burial."

Ryan shrugged. "OK," he said, "just as you like."

Then he turned and ordered a grave dug. Next he led Kildare, Cappy, Hazard, and Mohra to where some horses were tied.

It was a long, weary ride back to Tiahuanaco.

At the airport, Kildare learned that Wu Fang and his party had made a deal with a renegade American pilot to steal a transport plane and fly them back to the United States. When last seen, the plane had been headed north.

Kildare turned to Ryan. "What's the fastest army job you've got?"

"We've got a big Condor," Ryan told him, "that was headed for Chile as a bombing plane. We stopped it here when it came down to gas up, and we were going to ship it back to the United States."

"Is there any reason why it shouldn't go back now?" Kildare asked.

"No," came the answer.

"OK, then," Kildare said. "Get us a pilot and we'll be going."

"You mean now?" demanded Ryan. "Why, it's almost midnight."

"Now," Kildare said.

The pilot was procured. A few minutes later they droned off into the night air.

Hazard was happier than he had ever been before in his life. Mohra was free from Wu Fang at last and was here beside him.

When he awoke, he saw it was dawn. Cappy and Kildare were already awake. Kildare was up in the pilot's cockpit. Now and then he came back with information he had picked up over the wireless.

"I think we're catching up with them," Kildare said, as they stopped at an airdrome for gas.

Later they were out over the Caribbean Sea, headed for Cuba.

"We've sent orders to Havana to stop Wu Fang's plane when he lands there for gas," Kildare said.

But when they landed, they found there had been confusion concerning these orders, and that Wu Fang had left unmolested.

"We'll get him, all right, when we reach the States," Kildare said, confidently. "We should be right on his tail when we hit Jacksonville."

"We've sent orders to this airport to stop Wu Fang, and they must have him by this time," Kildare said at Jacksonville.

As they circled the field, they saw headlights from cars shining across the airport. In the light of the beams, they saw a dark blotch upon the field.

"Look!" Kildare shouted. "What's that? Looks like a plane has crashed out there with a broken landing gear."

They leaped from the Condor as it stopped.

"That's Wu Fang's plane all right," Kildare exclaimed. "Looks as though a police car ran into it and blocked its way. Come on."

As they ran, Hazard saw flashlight beams, three of them, playing about the ground.

"Are you the police I sent for?" Kildare asked.

"We sure are," they called back. "We tried to capture the plane, but it started to take off. One of our men drove a car in front of it and crashed it. He and two others were killed."

"How long ago did they land?" Kildare shouted.

"About five minutes ago."

"Have you captured anybody?" Kildare demanded.

"We got one bird," a police officer called back. "But if they all stink like he does, we don't want them in the Jacksonville jail."

"Turn on the floodlights," Kildare ordered. "Hasn't anybody got sense enough to light up the place?"

"They're out of order," the police told him. "We had a thunderstorm this evening and it put out all the lights."

Mohra and Hazard ran through the darkness after Kildare. Suddenly, the government man was lost to view. He must have turned in some other direction, Hazard decided.

The next instant, Kildare shouted, "Over here, Jerry! I got it! I've got the golden mask! Hurry! Here's Wu Fang, too."

Hazard turned. He ran wildly in the direction from which Kildare's voice came.

"Stop him! Stop him!" the government man was yelling. "Wu Fang has escaped!"

"**CONFOUND IT,**" Kildare swore as Hazard came running, "he was right here. I found him lying on the ground, must have been stunned in the crash. I snatched the yellow mask from his hand but was attacked from behind by one of his agents. When I managed to get to my feet, Wu Fang had disappeared."

"You've got the mask?" Hazard asked eagerly.

"No," Kildare cried, holding the gleaming object down at his side. "No, I haven't got the mask. That's my gun you see in my hand."

Aside he whispered, "Quiet, Jerry. Don't let on we've got the mask."

Hazard's thoughts had been on Kildare. He had taken it for

granted that Mohra was right behind him. Now, as he stared into blank darkness, he realized that she was not there. Panic seized him as he whirled. He dashed back along the path he had followed. No one there.

"Mohra, Mohra!" he shouted wildly. "Mohra, answer me!"

Not even the echo of his own voice came back to him. He heard someone running behind him. He turned, hoping it might be Mohra. It was Cappy.

"Have you seen Mohra?" he asked.

"Gee, no," said the boy. "I thought she was with you."

"She was," Hazard groaned. "I shouldn't have left her, but I thought Kildare was in trouble and—"

A great lump rose in his throat and choked off his words. He searched the airport until the dawn. There was no evidence of Mohra or Wu Fang or his agents.

As the great Condor roared north in the evening light, Kildare produced the yellow mask from the paper in which he had wrapped it. He studied it intently.

Hazard watched with disinterested eyes. Mohra's disappearance had so filled him with despair, he had little interest in what was going on around him.

At length, Kildare looked up. "I found little sponge-like formations around the inside of the eyes of the mask," he said. "It must have been those that contained the drug or whatever it was that possessed such hypnotic powers. The drug was probably obtained from the Cerrosa beetles that President Fierez told us about.

"But the mask's power is broken now, and it can do no more

harm. I tore out the spongy substance and burned it this morning. The mask of Unga is now but a beautiful example of the goldsmith's art and will henceforth repose in the Metropolitan museum."

Hazard made no comment. His eyes stared fixedly at the seat ahead.

"Come on, Jerry," Kildare urged. "Snap out of it. At least you can be sure of one thing now. Mohra's all for you, fellow. That should be worth a lot—

"Someday things will run a little more smoothly for you both. I'm sure of it. Besides, you've got to think of your real job. What a whale of a story you'll have for your syndicate!"

Hazard nodded mechanically, his eyes fixed on that seat.

"Yes," he said dully, "if I can ever bring myself to write it.

POPULAR PUBLICATIONS
HERO PULPS

LOOK FOR MORE SOON!

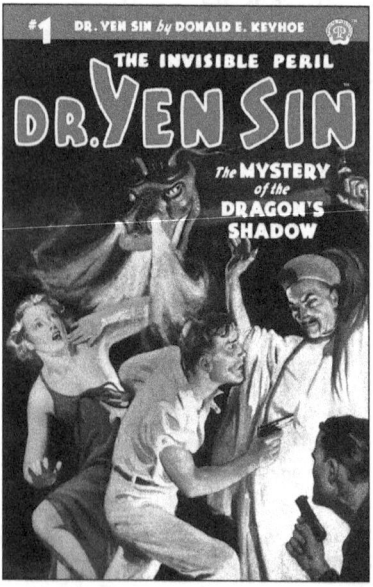

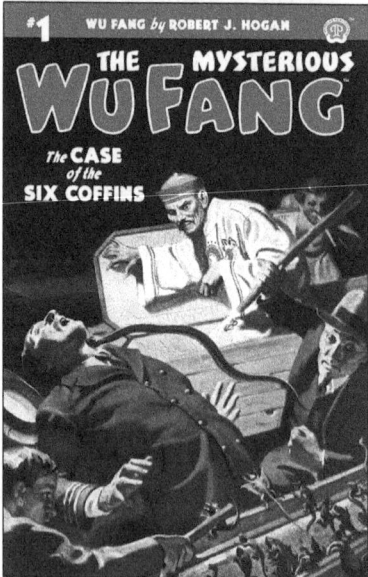